MY FAVOURITE
STORIES OF LAKELAND

My Favourite STORIES OF LAKELAND

edited by
MELVYN BRAGG

illustrated by
A. WAINWRIGHT
and by
PETER McCLURE

LUTTERWORTH PRESS
Guildford and London

First published in this collected form 1981
Introduction, choice of material and editorial links
copyright © 1981 by Melvyn Bragg

ISBN 0 7188 2396 6

Set in 12 point Bembo

Printed in Great Britain by
Butler & Tanner Ltd
Frome and London

Contents

★   ★   ★

ILLUSTRATIONS
by A. Wainwright

★   ★   ★

LINE DECORATIONS
by Peter McClure
   at all chapter heads excepting page 37

Acknowledgments

The editor and the publishers would like to express their gratitude to all who have granted permission for the inclusion of copyright material, or who have helped in the obtaining of that permission:

Oxford University Press, for permission to reprint the letter to Sara Hutchinson, August 6, 1802, from *Collected Letters of Samuel Taylor Coleridge*, edited by Earl Leslie Griggs, Vol. II (1956)

Frederick Warne & Co. Ltd, for permission to reprint the entries for July 26 to August 24, 1895, from *The Journal of Beatrix Potter*, transcribed by Leslie Linder, © copyright Frederick Warne & Co. Ltd, London

Mr Michael Moon, of the Beckermet Bookshop, Beckermet, and of Roper Street, Whitehaven, for permission to reprint an extract from *The Secret Valley* by Nicholas Size (originally published by Frederick Warne & Co. Ltd), reissued by him in his series of Cumbrian classics

Macmillan, London and Basingstoke, for permission to reprint the extract from *Rogue Herries* by Hugh Walpole

The University of Lancaster, for permission to reprint the interview of Mrs N.o.4. from *Working Class Barrow and Lancaster* by Dr Elizabeth Roberts

Collins, Publishers, for permission to reprint the extract from *North Star* by Graham Sutton

David Higham Associates Ltd, for permission to quote from *Provincial Pleasures* by Norman Nicholson, published by Robert Hale

The Arthur Ransome Estate, Mr Rupert Hart-Davis, and Jonathan Cape Ltd, for permission to reprint extracts from *The Autobiography of Arthur Ransome*, edited by Rupert Hart-Davis

Garnstone Press Ltd and Geoffrey Bles (Publishers) Ltd, for permission to reprint an extract from *The Shining Levels* by John Wyatt, published by Geoffrey Bles

Martin Secker & Warburg Ltd, for permission to reprint an extract from *The Hired Man* by Melvyn Bragg

Mr A. Wainwright, for permission to reprint extracts from *A Pictorial Guide to the Lakeland Fells*, published by the Westmorland Gazette, Kendal

Introduction

I have just come in from a walk around the foothills of the
Northern Fells. I did not go onto the mountains themselves,
wanting to be back home in time to have a few hours' stretch
for work. And there's been snow. Those docile white rumps
and seductive unblemished curves, that tantalising display of
glittering particles of ice so exquisite to crush under foot, all
the pleasing peaceful ease of these mantled hills is deceptive.
Each year claims its tragedies. More comfortable to be in the
cottage in front of a log fire with a pot of tea and a pen, to
watch the moon rise up at four in the afternoon and be quite
glad not to be out on what now looks like a magical silver
carpet draping itself languidly over harmless old contours.
The fells are treacherous.

To Daniel Defoe, one of the first travellers to write about
the area, it was a 'barren and frightful' place. The hills were
'monstrous high'; and 'they had a kind of inhospitable terror
in them'. Allowing for the more primitive state of the district
at that time—in the seventeen-twenties—and for the wonder
which townspeople at that time felt (or felt obliged to feel)
when they looked on raw Nature—there still seems to me
more truth of the place in Defoe's frightening descriptions
than in the bland and cheerful essays we tend to get nowa-
days. This place has been attractive to so many writers
because of its power. Perhaps Defoe exaggerated: but those
who affect to regard it as a hilly toyland are guilty of a much
greater error; lack of respect. The power is here—to excite
feelings both of beauty and fear.

After Defoe came William Gilpin in the seventeen-
seventies with his theories of 'Picturesque Beauty'. Gilpin
was Cumberland-born but spent most of his adult life as a
schoolmaster and parson in the south. The call of the native
hills was strong, however, as it so often is to those of us born
here (sentimental as that may sound) and Gilpin came back
home to make his observations on the viewing of nature as in
a frame. It was he who established the 'pretty-as-a-picture'
Lakes and since his time there has been a steady stream of

visitors and scholars looking over the place and describing it. Gilpin put the district on the tourist map at the time when tourism was beginning the first of many booms. Only about forty years later, the idea of visiting the district was suggested to Elizabeth Bennet in *Pride and Prejudice*: 'What are men to rocks and mountains' she rapturously cried. 'Oh what hours of transport we shall spend! And when we *do* return, it shall not be like other travellers, without giving one accurate idea of anything. We *will* know where we have gone—we *will* recollect what we have seen. Lakes, mountains and rivers shall not be jumbled together in our imaginations.' From Jane Austen it was an inevitable step to school-trips and now, in the holidays, the place is as warm with children intent on not jumbling together the lakes and mountains and rivers. As a picturesque and alluring bit of the map, then, with the special characteristic of almost infinite variety compacted within walkable boundaries, the Lake District has been a draw for two hundred years.

But at the end of the eighteenth century, William and Dorothy Wordsworth landed back in the county which had nurtured, delighted and tormented them in their childhoods —and the whole nature of the place changed. For Wordsworth transformed the Lake District from a mecca for tourists to a centre of poetry. He wrote about the place minutely so that everyone who comes to know his poetry comes to know the district. More importantly, he developed an idea of man's relationship with nature and with the sensations of his own past life which makes him one of the great philosopher-poets. He changed the way we look at the world. And the inspiration came from these few miles of rock and water.

So the Lake District became part of English literature and visitors now included Coleridge, Southey, De Quincey, Shelley, Keats, Lamb, Dickens, Sir Walter Scott, Charlotte and Branwell Brontë, Mrs Gaskell ... and from America, Emerson, Longfellow and Hawthorne. More potent even than Provence for the Impressionists, the Lake District, being the subject and object both of a great poet and of a profound revolution in poetry, ceased to be a local attraction and was shunted onto the mainline of literary life.

To compile a collection devoted to descriptions, from Gilpin's 'Picturesque' to William Rollinson's present-day work on the history and development of the area, would be fairly straightforward. To compile an anthology of poetry, from Wordsworth to Norman Nicholson, would be an equally untroubled task. But stories seemed to present a problem. Though rich in poetry and place, the area has been less well endowed with fiction. After some rather disappointing reading, I decided that 'stories' could include non-fiction. So much of it is so good that it seems a foolish waste to have it omitted for want of a tale. On the other hand, I have been sparing with the non-fiction: no Gilpin and no Hutchinson and no Canon Rawnsley, I'm afraid; and no poetry. The last restraint has been particularly severe when you consider that *The Prelude* has been described as the first and one of the finest autobiographies ever written. And the same even applies to *John Peel*, the most famous hunting song there is, written a few miles from where I sit, to celebrate the deeds of a man who hunted the fells I walk. But journals, diaries—if they hold a story—yes.

The result of this reading and sorting—with much help from Ron Sands—is now piled around me in photostats, paperbacks, first editions, only editions, popular editions, files and pamphlets. Outside there's a thaw on with occasional bursts of sleet as a reminder of hard times; inside there's more tea, more logs, the very best conditions for writing. And reading.

To
BILL ROLLINSON

I

That Lofty Solitude

WILLIAM WORDSWORTH

Wordsworth's Guide to the Lakes (1810), done as a money-spinner, still commands admiration for its clarity and usefulness. There's the famous description of the Lakes being laid out as the spokes of a wheel; there are the crusty prejudices; and there are times when he tells of a memorable walk. He does this here in the description of an excursion to the top of Scafell Pikes. The only philosophy belongs to the shepherd properly respected by Wordsworth. It's the story of a fine day observed by a man who knows his district and loves his outings. I cannot think of a better way to read yourself into the Lakes than through its greatest writer going up its highest mountain in his plainest prose.

Having left Rosthwaite in Borrowdale on a bright morning in the first week of October, we ascended from Seathwaite to the top of the ridge, called Ash-course [presumably Esk Hause]*, and thence beheld three distinct views;—on one side, the continuous Vale of Borrowdale, Keswick, and Bassenthwaite,—with Skiddaw, Helvellyn, Saddle-back, and numerous other mountains,—and, in the distance, the Solway Firth and the Mountains of Scotland;—on the other side, and below us, the Langdale Pikes—their own vale below *them*;—Windermere,—and, far beyond Windermere, Ingleborough in Yorkshire. But how shall I speak of the deliciousness of the third prospect! At this time, *that* was most favoured by sunshine and shade. The green Vale of Esk—deep and green, with its glittering serpent stream, lay below us; and on we looked to the Mountains near the Sea,—Black Comb

---

* The spellings of proper names, such as 'Scawfell', often vary slightly from those in modern use; major variants are noted in parentheses.

pre-eminent,—and, still beyond, to the Sea itself, in dazzling brightness. Turning round we saw the Mountains of Wastdale in tumult; to our right, Great Gavel [Great Gable], the loftiest, a distinct and *huge* form, though the middle of the mountain was, to our eyes, as its base.

We had attained the object of this journey; but our ambition now mounted higher. We saw the summit of Scawfell, apparently very near to us; and we shaped our course towards it; but, discovering that it could not be reached without first making a considerable descent, we resolved instead to aim at another point of the same mountain, called the *Pikes*, which I have since found has been estimated as higher than the summit bearing the name of Scawfell Head, where the Stone Man is built.

The sun had never once been overshadowed by a cloud during the whole of our progress from the centre of Borrowdale. On the summit of the Pike, which we gained after much toil, though without difficulty, there was not a breath of air to stir even the papers containing our refreshments, as they lay spread out upon a rock. The stillness seemed to be not of this world:—we paused, and kept silence to listen; and no sound could be heard: the Scawfell Cataracts were voiceless to us; and there was not an insect to hum in the air. The vales which we had seen from Ash-course lay yet in view; and side by side with Eskdale we now saw the sister Vale of Donnerdale terminated by the Duddon Sands. But the majesty of the mountains below, and close to us, is not to be conceived. We now beheld the whole mass of Great Gavel from its base,— the Den of Wastdale at our feet—a gulf immeasurable; Grasmere and the other mountains of Crummock; Ennerdale and its mountains; and the Sea beyond! We sat down to our repast, and gladly would we have tempered our beverage (for there was no spring or well near us) with such a supply of delicious water as we might have procured had we been on the rival summit of Great Gavel; for on its highest point is a small triangular receptacle in the native rock, which, the shepherds say, is never dry. There we might have slaked our thirst plenteously with a pure and celestial liquid, for the cup or basin, it appears, has no other feeder than the dews of heaven, the showers, the vapours, the hoar frost, and the spotless snow.

Solway coastal plain

Skiddaw — Saddleback (Blencathra)

← COCKERMOUTH — Bassenthwaite

Vale of Lorton — Whinlatter Pass — KESWICK — PENRITH →

Buttermere — Crummock Water — Newlands — Borrowdale — Thirlmere — Helvellyn — Ullswater — PENRITH →

PATTERDALE

Ennerdale Water — Ennerdale — Honister Pass — Rosthwaite — Seathwaite — Kirkstone Pass

Great Gable — Langdale Pikes — GRASMERE

Scafell Pikes — Esk House — Langdale — AMBLESIDE

Wastwater — Scafell — Hardknott Pass — Wrynose Pass — KENDAL →

Wasdale — Eskdale — Dunnerdale — CONISTON — Windermere — WINDERMERE

Black Combe — Broughton-in-Furness — Coniston Water — NEWBY BRIDGE

MILLOM — BARROW-IN-FURNESS → — Furness — ULVERSTON — LANCASTER →

Irish Sea — Duddon

looking north

While we were gazing around, 'Look,' I exclaimed, 'at yon ship upon the glittering sea!' 'Is it a ship?' replied our shepherd-guide. 'It can be nothing else,' interposed my companion; 'I cannot be mistaken, I am so accustomed to the appearance of ships at sea.' The Guide dropped the argument; but before a minute was gone he quietly said, 'Now look at your ship; it is changed into a horse.' So indeed it was,—a horse with a gallant neck and head. We laughed heartily; and, I hope, when again inclined to be positive, I may remember the ship and the horse upon the glittering sea; and the calm confidence, yet submissiveness, of our wise Man of the Mountains, who certainly had more knowledge of clouds than we, whatever might be our knowledge of ships.

I know not how long we might have remained on the summit of the Pike, without a thought of moving, had not our Guide warned us that we must not linger; for a storm was coming. We looked in vain to espy the signs of it. Mountains, vales, and sea were touched with the clear light of the sun. 'It is there,' said he, pointing to the sea beyond Whitehaven, and there we perceived a light vapour unnoticeable but by a shepherd accustomed to watch all mountain bodings. We gazed around again, and yet again, unwilling to lose the remembrance of what lay before us in that lofty solitude; and then prepared to depart. Meanwhile the air changed to cold, and we saw that tiny vapour swelled into mighty masses of cloud which came boiling over the mountains. Great Gavel, Helvellyn, and Skiddaw, were wrapped in storm; yet Langdale, and the mountains in that quarter, remained all bright in sunshine. Soon the storm reached us; we sheltered under a crag; and almost as rapidly as it had come it passed away, and left us free to observe the struggles of gloom and sunshine in other quarters. Langdale now had its share, and the Pikes of Langdale were decorated by two splendid rainbows. Skiddaw also had his own rainbows. Before we again reached Ash-course every cloud had vanished from every summit.

I ought to have mentioned that round the top of Scawfell-Pike not a blade of grass is to be seen. Cushions or tufts of moss, parched and brown, appear between the huge blocks and stones that lie in heaps on all sides to a great distance, like skeletons or bones of the earth not needed at the creation, and there left to be covered with never-dying lichens, which the clouds and dews nourish; and adorn with colours of vivid and exquisite beauty. Flowers, the most brilliant feathers, and even gems, scarcely surpass in colouring some of those masses of stone, which no human eye beholds, except the shepherd or traveller be led thither by curiosity: and how seldom must this happen! For the other eminence is the one visited by the adventurous stranger; and the shepherd has no inducement to ascend the PIKE in quest of his sheep; no food being *there* to tempt them.

We certainly were singularly favoured in the weather; for when we were seated on the summit, our conductor, turning his eyes thoughtfully round, said, 'I do not know that in my whole life I was ever, at any season of the year, so high upon the mountains on so *calm* a day.' (It was the seventh of October.) Afterwards we had a spectacle of the grandeur of earth and heaven commingled; yet without terror. We knew that the storm would pass away, for so our prophetic Guide had assured us.

Before we reached Seathwaite in Borrowdale, a few stars had appeared, and we pursued our way down the Vale, to Rosthwaite, by moonlight.

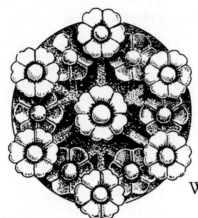

2

The Beauty of Buttermere

or Tragedy in Real Life

WILSON ARMISTEAD

In 1802, in the valley of Buttermere, then as isolated as Tibet, there was a young woman called Mary. On a trip to the Lakes, an idle London sketcher and scribbler wrote and published an account of her beauty. Her father was a small farmer who kept an ale-house which was subsequently sniffed out by men of fashion who wanted to glimpse the Beauty of Buttermere. Even Wordsworth rambled across there and wrote some lines about her. Then the Honourable Alexander Augustus Hope came on the scene. . . . In this version of the story, the account of Mary's reputation before 'Hope' encountered her is left out. The writer, despite himself, was obviously fascinated by her seducer.

JOHN HATFIELD, who acquired the appellation of the Keswick Imposter, and whose extraordinary villainy excited universal hatred, was born in [or before] 1759, at Mottram, in Cheshire, of low parentage, but possessing great natural abilities. His face was handsome, his person genteel, his eyes blue, and his complexion fair.

After some domestic depredations—for in his early days he betrayed an iniquitous disposition—he quitted his family, and was employed as traveller to a linen-draper in the north of England. In the course of this service, he became acquainted with a young woman, who was nursed, and resided at, a farmer's house in the neighbourhood of his employer. She had been, in her earlier life, taught to consider the people with whom she lived as her parents. Remote from the gaieties and follies of polished life, she was unacquainted with the allurements of fashion, and considered her domestic duties as the only object of her consideration. When this deserving girl had arrived at a certain age, the honest farmer explained to her the secret of her birth; he told her, that, notwithstanding she had always considered him as her parent, he was, in fact, only her poor guardian; and that she was the natural daughter of Lord Robert Manners, who intended to give her £1,000, provided she married with his approbation.

This discovery soon reached the ears of Hatfield; he immediately paid his respects at the farmer's, and having represented himself as a young man of considerable expectations in the wholesale linen business, his visits were not discountenanced. The farmer, however, thought it incumbent on him to acquaint his lordship with a proposal made to him by Hatfield, that he would marry the young woman, if her relations were satisfied with their union, but on no other terms. This had so much the appearance of an honourable and prudent intention, that his lordship, on being made acquainted with the circumstances, desired to see the lover. He accordingly paid his respects to the noble and unsuspecting parent who, conceiving the young man to be what he represented himself, gave his consent at the first interview; and, the day after the marriage took place, presented the bridegroom with a draft on his banker for £1,500. This took place about 1771 or 1772.

Shortly after the receipt of his lordship's bounty, Hatfield set off for London; hired a small phaeton; was perpetually at the coffee-houses in Covent Garden; described himself to whatever company he chanced to meet, as a near relation of the Rutland family; vaunted of his parks and hounds; but as great liars have seldom good memories, he so varied in his descriptive figures, that he acquired the appellation of *Lying Hatfield*.

The marriage portion now exhausted, he retreated from London, and was scarcely heard of for about ten years, when he again visited the metropolis, having left his wife, with three daughters, to depend on the precarious charity of her relations. Happily, she did not long survive; and the author of her calamities, during his stay in London, soon experienced calamity himself, having been arrested, and committed to

King's Bench prison, for a debt amounting to the sum of £160. Several unfortunate gentlemen, then confined in the same place, had been of his parties when he flourished in Covent Garden, and perceiving him in great poverty, frequently invited him to dinner; yet such was his unaccountable disposition, that notwithstanding he knew there were people present who were thoroughly acquainted with his character, still he would continue to describe his Yorkshire park, his estate in Rutlandshire, settled upon his wife, and generally wind up the whole with observing how vexatious it was to be confined at the suit of a paltry tradesman for so insignificant a sum, at the very moment when he had thirty men employed in cutting a piece of water near the family mansion in Yorkshire.

At the time Hatfield became a prisoner in the King's Bench, the unfortunate Valentine Morris, formerly governor of St Vincent's, was confined in the same place. This gentleman was frequently visited by a clergyman of the most benevolent and humane disposition. Hatfield soon directed his attention to this good man, and one day earnestly invited to attend him to his chamber; after some preliminary apologies, he implored the worthy pastor never to disclose what he was going to communicate. The divine assured him the whole should remain in his bosom. 'Then,' said Hatfield, 'you see before you a man nearly allied to the house of Rutland, and possessed of estates (here followed the old story of the Yorkshire park, the Rutlandshire property, &c., &c.,); yet notwithstanding all this wealth,' continued he, 'I am detained in this wretched place for the insignificant sum of £160. But the truth is, Sir, I would not have my situation known to any man in the world but my worthy relative, his Grace of Rutland. Indeed, I would rather remain a captive for ever. If you would have the goodness to pay your respects to this worthy nobleman, and frankly describe how matters are, he will at once send me the money by you; and this mighty business will not only be instantly settled, but I shall have the satisfaction of introducing you to a connection which may be attended with happy consequences.'

The honest clergyman readily undertook the commission; paid his respects to the Duke, and pathetically described the unfortunate situation of his amiable relative. His Grace of

Rutland, not recollecting at the moment such a name as Hatfield, expressed his astonishment at the application. This reduced the worthy divine to a very awkward situation, and he faltered in his speech, when he began making an apology; which the Duke perceiving, he very kindly observed, that he believed the whole was some idle tale of an imposter, for that he never knew any person of the name mentioned, although he had some faint recollection of hearing Lord Robert Manners, his relation, say that he had married a natural daughter of his to a tradesman in the north of England, and whose name he believed was Hatfield.

The Reverend was so confounded that he immediately retired and proceeded to the prison, where he gave the imposter, in the presence of Mr Morris, a most severe lecture. But the appearance of this venerable man, as his friend, had the effect which Hatfield expected; for the Duke sent to inquire if he was the man that married the natural daughter of Lord Robert Manners, and, being satisfied as to the fact, despatched a messenger with £200, and had him released.

In 1784, his Grace of Rutland was appointed Lord Lieutenant of Ireland; and shortly after his arrival in Dublin, Hatfield made his appearance in that city. He immediately, on his landing, engaged a suite of rooms at a hotel in College Green, and represented himself as nearly allied to the Viceroy, but that he could not appear at the castle until his horses, servants, and carriages were arrived, which he ordered, before leaving England, to be shipped at Liverpool. The easy and familiar manner in which he addressed the master of the hotel, perfectly satisfied him that he had a man of consequence in his house, and matters were arranged accordingly. This being adjusted, Hatfield soon found his way to Lucas's coffee-house, a place which people of a certain rank generally frequent; and, it being a new scene, the Yorkshire park, the Rutlandshire estate, and the connection with the Rutland family, stood their ground very well for about a month.

At the expiration of this time, the bill at the hotel amounted to £60 and upwards. The landlord became importunate, and after expressing his astonishment at the non-arrival of Mr Hatfield's domestics, etc., requested he might be permitted to send in his bill. This did not in the least confuse Hatfield; he immediately told the master of the hotel, that very unfortunately his agent, who received the rents of his estates in the north of England, was then in Ireland, and held a public employment; he lamented that his agent was not then in Dublin, but he had the pleasure to know his stay in the country would not exceed three days. This satisfied the landlord; and at the expiration of the three days, he called upon the gentleman whose name Hatfield had given him, and presented the account. Here followed another scene of confusion and surprise. The supposed agent of the Yorkshire estate very frankly told the man who delivered the bill, that he had no other knowledge of the person who sent him than what common report furnished him with, that his general character in London was that of a romantic simpleton whose plausibilities had imposed on several people, and plunged himself into repeated difficulties.

The landlord retired, highly thankful for the information, and immediately arrested his guest who was lodged in the prison of the Marshalsea. Hatfield had scarcely seated himself in his new lodgings, when he visited the jailer's wife in her apartment, and in a whisper, requested of her not to tell any person that she had in her custody a near relation of the then Viceroy. The woman, astonished at the discovery, immediately showed him into the best apartment in the prison, had a table provided, and she, her husband, and Hatfield, constantly dined together, for nearly three weeks, in the utmost harmony and good humour.

During this time he had petitioned the Duke for another supply, who, apprehensive that the fellow might continue his impositions in Dublin, released him, on condition of his immediately quitting Ireland; and his Grace sent a servant, who conducted him on board the packet that sailed the next tide for Holyhead.

In 1792, he came to Scarbro', introduced himself to the acquaintance of several persons of distinction in that neighbourhood, and insinuated that he was, by the interest of the Duke of Rutland, soon to be one of the representatives in parliament for the town of Scarbro'. After several weeks' stay at the principal inn, his imposture was detected by his inability to pay the bill. Soon after his arrival in London, he was arrested for this debt, and thrown into prison. He had been eight years and a half in confinement, when a Miss

Nation, of Devonshire, to whom he had become known, paid his debts, took him from prison, and gave him her hand in marriage.

Soon after he was liberated, he had the good fortune to prevail with some highly respectable merchants in Devonshire to take him into partnership with them; and, with a clergyman to accept his drafts to a large amount. He made upon this foundation a splendid appearance in London; and, before the general election, even proceeded to canvass the rotten burgh of Queenborough. Suspicions in the meantime arose, in regard to his character, and the state of his fortune. He retired from the indignation of his creditors, and was declared a bankrupt, in order to bring his villainies to light. Thus, having left behind his second wife and two infant children at Tiverton, he visited other places; and, at length, in July, 1802, arrived at the Queen's Head in Keswick, in a handsome travelling carriage, but without any servant, where he assumed the name of the Hon. Alexander Augustus Hope, brother of the Earl of Hopetoun, M.P., for Linlithgow.

From Keswick, as his head-quarters, he made excursions in every direction amongst the neighbouring valleys; meeting, generally, a good deal of respect and attention, partly on account of his handsome equipage, and still more from his visiting cards, which designated him as 'the Honourable Alexander Augustus Hope.' Some persons had discernment enough to doubt of this; for his breeding and deportment, though showy, had a tinge of vulgarity about it; he was grossly ungrammatical in his ordinary conversation. He received letters under this assumed name—which might be through collusion with accomplices—but he himself continually franked letters by that name. That being a capital offence, not only a forgery, but (as a forgery on the post-office) sure to be prosecuted, nobody presumed to question his pretensions any longer; and henceforward, he went to all places with the consideration attached to an earl's brother. All doors flew open at his approach; boats, boatmen, nets, and the most unlimited sporting privileges, were placed at the disposal of the 'Honourable' gentleman; and the hospitality of the whole country taxed itself to offer a suitable reception to the patrician Scotchman.

Nine miles from Keswick, by the nearest route, lies the

lake of Buttermere. Its margin, which is overhung by some
of the loftiest and steepest of Cumbrian mountains, exhibits
on either side few traces of human neighbourhood; the level
area, where the hills recede enough to allow of any, is of a
wild, pastoral character, or almost savage; the waters of the
lake are deep and sullen; and the barrier mountains, by
excluding the sun for much of its daily course, strengthen
the gloomy impressions. At the foot of this lake (that is, at
the end where its waters issue), lie a few unornamented fields,
through which rolls a little brook-like river, connecting it
with the larger lake of Crummock; and at the edge of this
little domain, upon the roadside, stands a cluster of cottages,
so small and few, that, in the richer tracts of the islands, they
would scarcely be complimented with the name of hamlet.
One of these, the principal, belonged to an independent pro-
prietor, called, in the local dialect, a 'Statesman;' and more,
perhaps, for the sake of gathering any little local news, than
with much view to pecuniary profit at that era, this cottage
offered the accommodations of an inn to traveller and his
horse.

Rare, however, must have been the mounted traveller in
those days, unless visiting Buttermere for itself, for the road
led to no further habitations of man, with the exception of
some four or five pastoral cabins, equally humble, in Gatesgarth dale. Hither, however, in an evil hour for the peace of
this little brotherhood of shepherds, came the cruel spoiler
from Keswick, and directed his steps to the once happy
cottage of poor Mary, the daughter of Mr and Mrs Robinson,
an old couple, who kept the inn, and had, by their industry,
gained a little property. She was the only daughter, and
probably her name had never been known to the public, but
for the account given of her by the author of *A Fortnight's
Ramble to the Lakes in Westmorland, Lancashire, and Cumberland.*

Hatfield now became acquainted with an Irish gentleman,
an M.P., who had been resident with his family some months
at Keswick. With this gentleman, and under his immediate
protection, there was likewise a young lady of family and
fortune, and of great personal attractions. One of the means
which Hatfield used to introduce himself to this respectable
family was the following:—Understanding that the gentleman had been a military man, he took an army list from his

pocket, and pointed to his assumed name, the Honourable Alexander Augustus Hope, lieutenant-colonel of the 14th regiment of foot. This new acquaintance daily gained strength; and he shortly paid his addresses to the daughter of the above gentleman, and obtained her consent. The wedding clothes were bought; but previously to the wedding-day being fixed, she insisted that the pretended Colonel Hope should introduce the subject formally to her friends. He now pretended to write letters; and, while waiting for the answers, proposed to employ that time in a trip to Lord Hopetoun's seat, &c.

From this time he played a double game; his visits to Keswick became frequent, and his suit to the young lady assiduous and fervent. Still, however, both at Keswick and Buttermere, he was somewhat shy of appearing in public. He was sure to be engaged in a fishing expedition on the day on which any company was expected at the public house at Buttermere; and he never attended the church at Keswick but once.

Finding his schemes baffled to obtain this young lady and her fortune, he now applied himself wholly to gain possession of Mary Robinson, who was a fine young woman of eighteen, and acted as waiter. In a situation so solitary, the stranger had unlimited facilities for enjoying her company, and recommending himself to her favour. Among the neighbours he made the most minute inquiries into every circumstance relating to her and her family. Doubts about his pretensions never arose in so simple a place as this; they were over-ruled before they could well have arisen, by the opinion now general in Keswick, that he really was what he pretended to be; and thus, with little demure, except in the shape of a few natural words of parting anger from a defeated or rejected rustic admirer, the young woman gave her hand in marriage to the showy and unprincipled stranger. He procured a licence, and they were married in the church of Lorton, on the 2nd of October, 1802. A romantic account of the circumstance found its way almost immediately into the newspapers. It thus fell under the notice of various individuals in Scotland, who knew that Colonel Hope, who was said to have married the flower of Buttermere, had been abroad the whole summer, and was now residing in Vienna.

Mr Charles Hope, then Lord Justice Clerk, afterwards
President of the Court of Session (a son-in-law of the Earl
of Hopetoun), made the fact known, and prompted
inquiries which led to the detection of the imposture.

On the day previous to his marriage, Hatfield wrote to
Mr Mansfield, informing him, that he was under the necessity of being absent for ten days on a journey into
Scotland, and sent him a draft for thirty pounds, drawn on
Mr Crumpt, of Liverpool, desired him to cash it, and pay
some small debts in Keswick with it, and send him over the
balance, as he feared he might be short of cash on the road.
This Mr Mansfield immediately did, and sent him ten guineas
in addition to the balance. On that Saturday, Wood, the landlord of the Queen's Head, returned from Lorton with the
public intelligence, that Colonel Hope had married the
Beauty of Buttermere. As it was clear, whoever he was, that
he had acted unworthily and dishonourably, Mr Mansfield's
suspicions were of course awakened. He instantly remitted
the draft to Mr Crumpt, who immediately accepted it. Mr
Mansfield wrote to the Earl of Hopetoun. Before the answer
arrived, the pretended honourable returned with his wife to
Buttermere. He went only as far as Longtown, when he
received two letters, seemed much troubled that some friends
whom he had expected had not arrived there, stayed three
days, and then told his wife that he would again go back to
Buttermere.

From this she was seized with fears and suspicions. They
returned, however, and their return was made known at
Keswick. The late Mr Harding, the barrister, and a Welsh
judge, passing through Keswick, heard of this imposter, and
sent his servant over to Buttermere with a note to the supposed Colonel Hope, who observed, 'that it was a mistake,
and that it was for a brother of his.' However, he sent for
four horses, and came over to Keswick; drew another draft
on Mr Crumpt for twenty pounds, which the landlord at the
Queen's Head had the courage to cash. Of this sum he immediately sent the ten guineas to Mr Mansfield, who came
and introduced him to the judge, as his old friend Colonel
Hope. But he made a blank denial that he had ever assumed
the name. He had said his name was Hope, but not that he was
the honourable member for Linlithgow, &c., &c.; and one

who had been his frequent intimate at Buttermere gave evidence to the same purpose.

In spite, however, of his impudent assertions, and those of his associate, the evidence against him was decisive. A warrant was given by Sir Frederick Vane on the clear proof of his having forged and received several franks as the member for Linlithgow; and he was committed to the care of a constable, but allowed to fish on the lake. Having, however, found means to escape, he took refuge for a few days on board a sloop off Ravenglass, and then went in the coach to Ulverston, and was afterwards seen at a hotel in Chester. In the meantime [an] advertisement, setting forth his person and manners was in the public prints.

Besides blighting the prospects of the poor [Mary], he had nearly ruined her father by running up a debt of eighteen pounds. His dressing-case, a very elegant piece of furniture, was left behind, and on being opened at Keswick by warrant of a magistrate, was found to contain every article that the most luxurious gentleman could desire, but no papers tending to discover his real name. Afterwards, Mary herself, searching more narrowly, discovered that the box had a double bottom, and in the intermediate recess, found a number of letters addressed to him by his wife and children under the name of Hatfield. The story of the deception immediately became as notorious as the marriage had been.

Though he was personally known in Cheshire to many of the inhabitants, yet this specious hypocrite had so artfully disguised himself, that he quitted the town without any suspicions before the Bow Street officers reached that place in quest of him. He was then traced to Brielth, in Brecknockshire, and was at length apprehended about sixteen miles from Swansea, and committed to Brecon jail. He had a cravat on, with his initials, J. H., which he attempted to account for by calling himself John Henry.

Before the magistrates he declared himself to be Ludor Henry; and in order to prepossess the honest Cambrians in his favour, boasted that he was descended from an ancient family in Wales, for the inhabitants of which country he had ever entertained a sincere regard. He was, however, conveyed up to town by the Bow Street officers, where he was examined on his arrival before the magistrates. The solicitor for his bankruptcy attended to identify his person, and stated, that the commission of bankruptcy was issued against Hatfield in June, 1802; that he attended the last meeting of the commissioners, but the prisoner did not appear, although due notice had been given in the *Gazette*, and he himself had given notice to the prisoner's wife, at Wakefield near Tiverton, Devon. Mr Parkyn, the solicitor to the Post-office, produced a warrant from Sir Frederick Vane, Bart., a magistrate for the county of Cumberland, against the prisoner, by the name of the Hon. Alexander Augustus Hope, charging him with felony, by pretending to be a member of parliament of the United Kingdom, and franking several letters by the name of A. Hope, to several persons, which were put into the Post-office at Keswick, in Cumberland, in order to evade the duties of postage. Another charge for forgery, and the charge for bigamy, were explained to him, but not entered into, as he was committed for trial for these charges at the next assizes at Carlisle. He conducted himself with the greatest propriety during his journey to town, and on his examination; but said nothing more than answering a few questions put to him by Sir Richard Ford and the solicitors, affecting to consider himself a persecuted individual, and representing, in particular, that, in the alliance with Mary Robinson, he had been rather sinned against than sinning. Mary, on the other hand, who was now announced to be likely to bear a child to her pretended husband, refused to become accessory to his prosecution. The utmost she could be prevailed on to do against Hatfield was to address the following letter to Sir Richard Ford:—

'The man whom I had the misfortune to marry, and who has ruined me and my aged parents, always told me he was the Hon. Colonel Hope, the next brother of the Earl of Hopetoun. Your grateful and unfortunate servant,

Mary Robinson.'

Mary's letter was read aloud in open court on December 27th. Its delicacy of sentiment moved all who heard it save Hatfield himself, who showed no contrition whatever. He was remanded for further examination, in the course of which a letter, signed and

franked 'A. Hope', and written from Buttermere on October 1,
1802, to Mr Crumpt, was produced, and proved to have passed free
of postage. A letter from his wife in Tiverton, and the certificate
of his marriage to Mary of Buttermere, were also produced. On
August 15, 1803, at the Assizes for Cumberland, Hatfield was
charged before the Honourable Alexander Thompson, on three
indictments, relating to his assumption of the name of Alexander
Augustus Hope. He pleaded not guilty.

Mr Scarlett opened the case in an address to the jury; and
gave an ample detail of the prisoner's guilt.

In support of what he had advanced, he called Mr Quick,
who was clerk in the house at Tiverton where Hatfield was
partner, who swore to his hand-writing. The Rev. Mr
Nicholson swore that when the prisoner was asked his name,
he said it was a comfortable one—Hope.

The evidence for the prosecution having closed, the
prisoner addressed himself to the jury. He said he felt some
degree of satisfaction in being able to have his sufferings
terminated, as they must of course be by their verdict. For
the space of nine months he had been dragged from prison
to prison, and torn from place to place, subject to all the
misrepresentations of calumny.

'Whatever will be my fate,' said he, 'I am content; it is
the award of justice, impartially and virtuously administered.
But I will solemnly declare that in all my transactions, I
never intended to defraud or injure the persons whose names
have appeared in the prosecution. This I will maintain to the
last of my life.'

After the evidence was gone through, his lordship, Sir A.
Thompson, summed up the whole of the evidence and com-
mented upon such parts as peculiarly affected the fate of the
prisoner. 'Nothing,' said his lordship, 'could be more clearly
proved, than that the prisoner did make the bill or bills in
question under the assumed name of Alexander Augustus
Hope, with an intention to defraud. That the prisoner used
the additional name of Augustus was of no consequence in
this question. The evidence proved clearly that the prisoner
meant to represent himself to be another character; and under
that assumed character, he drew the bills in question. If anything should appear in mitigation of the offences with which

the prisoner was charged, they must give them a full consideration; and though his character had been long shaded with obloquy, yet they must not let this in the least influence the verdict they were sworn to give.'

The jury consulted about ten minutes, and then returned a verdict—Guilty of Forgery.

During the whole of the trial the court was excessively crowded. The prisoner's behaviour was proper and dignified; and he supported his situation from first to last with unshaken fortitude. He employed himself during the greatest part of his trial, in writing notes on the evidence given, and in conversing with his counsel.

When the verdict of the jury was given, he manifested no relaxation of his accustomed demeanour. After the court adjourned, he retired from the bar, and was ordered to attend the next morning to receive the sentence of the law. The crowd was immense; and he was allowed a post-chaise from the town-hall to the jail.

At eight o'clock the next morning, the court met again, when the prisoner appeared at the bar to receive his sentence. Numbers of people gathered together to witness this painful duty of the law passed upon one whose appearance, manners, and actions, had excited a most uncommon degree of interest. After proceeding in the usual form, the judge addressed the prisoner in the following impressive terms:—

'John Hatfield, after the long and serious investigation of the charges which have been preferred against you, you have been found guilty by a jury of your country. You have been distinguished for crimes of such magnitude, as have seldom, if ever, received any mitigation of capital punishment; and in your case, it is impossible it can be limited. Assuming the person, name, and character, of a worthy and respectable officer of a noble family in this country, you have perpetrated and committed the most enormous crimes. The long imprisonment you have undergone has afforded time for your serious reflection, and an opportunity for your being deeply impressed with a sense of the enormity of your crimes, and the justness of that sentence which must be inflicted upon you; and I wish you to be seriously impressed with the awfulness of your situation. I conjure you to reflect with anxious care and deep concern on your approaching end, concerning which much remains to be done. Lay aside now your delusions and impositions, and employ properly the short space you have to live. I beseech you to employ the remaining part of your time in preparing for eternity, so that you may find mercy at the hour of death, and in the day of judgment. Hear, now, the sentence of the law:—That you be carried from hence to the place from whence you came, and from thence to the place of execution, and there to be hung by the neck till you are dead; and may the Lord have mercy on your soul!'

A notion very generally prevailed that he would not be brought to justice; and the arrival of the mail was daily expected with the greatest impatience. No pardon arriving, Saturday, September 3, 1803, was at last fixed upon for the execution.

The gallows was erected the preceding night, between twelve and three, on an island formed by the river Eden, on the north side of the town, between the two bridges. From the hour when the jury found him guilty, he behaved with the utmost serenity and cheerfulness. He talked upon the topics of the day with the greatest interest or indifference. He could scarcely ever be brought to speak of his own case. He neither blamed the verdict, nor made any confession of his guilt. He said he had no intention to defraud those whose names he forged; but was never heard to say that he was to die unjustly. None of his relations ever visited him during his confinement.

The alarming nature of the crime of forgery, in a commercial country, had taught him, from the beginning, to entertain no hope of mercy. By ten in the morning of September 3, his irons were struck off; he appeared as usual, and no one observed any alteration or increased agitation whatever.

Soon after ten o'clock he sent for the *Carlisle Journal*, and perused it for some time. A little after he had laid aside the paper, two clergymen (Mr Pattison of Carlisle and Mr Mark of Burgh-on-Sands), attended and prayed with him for about two hours, and drank coffee with him. After they left him, about twelve, he wrote some letters, and in one he enclosed his penknife; it was addressed to London. About this time he also shaved himself; though intrusted with a razor, he never seems to have meditated an attempt upon his life; but it was generally reported on Friday night that he had poisoned himself, though without foundation. To all who spoke with him, he pretended that what he had to suffer was a matter of little consequence. He preferred talking on indifferent subjects. At three, he dined with the jailer, and ate heartily. Having taken a glass or two of wine, he ordered coffee. He took a cup a few minutes before he set out for the place of execution. The last thing he did was to read a chapter from the 2d Corinthians. He had previously marked out this passage for his lesson before he was to mount the scaffold.

The sheriffs, the bailiffs, and the Carlisle volunteer cavalry, attended at the jail door about half-past three, together with a post-chaise and hearse. He was then ordered into the turnkey's lodge, for the purpose of being pinioned, where he inquired of the jailer, who were going in the chaise with him? He was told the executioner and the jailer. He immediately said, 'Pray, where is the executioner? I should wish much to see him.' The executioner was sent for. Hatfield asked him how he was, and made him a present of some silver in a paper. During the time of his being pinioned, he stood with resolution, and requested he might not be pinioned tight, as he wished to use his handkerchief on the platform; which was complied with. A prodigious crowd had assembled; this was the market day, and people had come from the distance of many miles out of mere curiosity. Hatfield, when he left the prison, wished all his fellow-prisoners might be happy; he then took farewell of the clergymen, who attended him to the door of the chaise, and mounted the steps with much steadiness and composure. The jailer and executioner went in along with him. The latter had been brought from Dumfries upon a retaining fee of ten guineas.

It was exactly four o'clock when the procession moved from the jail. Passing through the Scotch gate, in about twelve minutes it arrived at the Sands. Half the yeomanry went before the carriage, and the other half behind. Upon arriving on the ground, they formed a ring round the scaffold. It is said that he wished to have the blinds drawn up, but that such an indulgence was held inconsistent with the interest of public justice. When he came in sight of the tree, he said to the jailer, he imagined that was the tree (pointing at it) that he was to die on. On being told yes, he exclaimed, 'O! a happy sight—I see it with pleasure!'

As soon as the carriage-door had been opened by the under-sheriff, he alighted with his two companions. A small-cart, boarded over, had been placed under the gibbet, and a ladder was placed against it, which he instantly ascended. He was dressed in a black jacket, black silk waistcoat, fustian pantaloons, shoes, and white cotton stockings. He was perfectly cool and collected. At the same time, his conduct displayed nothing of levity, of insensibility, or of hardihood. He was more anxious to give proof of resignation than of heroism. His countenance was extremely pale, but his hand never trembled. He immediately untied his neckerchief, and placed a bandage over his eyes. Then he desired the hangman, who was extremely awkward, to be as expert as possible about it, and that he would wave a handkerchief when he was ready. The hangman not having fixed the rope in its proper place, he put up his hand and turned it himself. He also tied his cap, took his handkerchief from his own neck, and tied it about his head also. Then he requested the jailer would step on the platform and pinion his arms a little harder, saying, that when he had lost his senses he might attempt to lift them to his neck. The rope was completely fixed about five minutes before five o'clock; it was slack, and he merely said, 'May the Almighty bless you all.' Nor did he falter in the least, when he tied the cap, shifted the rope, and took his handkerchief from his neck.

He several times put on a languid and piteous smile. He at last seemed rather exhausted and faint. Having been near three weeks under sentence of death, he must have suffered much, notwithstanding his external bearing; and a reflection of the misery he had occasioned must have given him many an agonizing throb.

Having taken leave of the jailer and sheriff, he prepared himself for his fate. He was at this time heard to exclaim, 'My spirit is strong, though my body is weak.'

Great apprehensions were entertained that it would be necessary to tie him up for a second time. The noose slipped twice, and he fell down about eighteen inches. His feet at the last were almost touching the ground; but his excessive weight, which occasioned this accident, speedily relieved him from pain. He expired in a moment, and without any struggle. The ceremony of his hands being tied behind his back, was satisfied by a piece of white tape passed loosely from one to the other; but he never made the smallest effort to relieve himself. He had calculated so well, that his money lasted exactly to the scaffold. As they were setting out, the hangman was going to search him. He threw him half-a-crown, saying,

'This is all my pockets contain.'

He had been in considerable distress before he received a supply from his father. He afterwards lived in great style, frequently making presents to his fellow felons. He was considered in the jail as a kind of emperor; he was allowed to do whatever he pleased, and no one took offence at the air of superiority which he assumed.

He was cut down after he had hung about an hour. On the preceding Wednesday he had applied to one of the clergymen who attended him, to recommend him a tradesman to make his coffin. Mr Bushby, of Carlisle, took measure of him. He did not appear at all agitated while Mr Bushby was so employed; but told him that he wished the coffin to be a strong oak one, plain and neat.

'I request, Sir,' he added, 'that after I am taken down, I may be put into the coffin immediately, with the apparel I may have on, and afterwards closely screwed down, put into the hearse which will be in waiting, carried to the churchyard, and be interred in the evening.'

A spot was fixed upon in a distant corner of the churchyard, far from the other tombs. No priest attended, and the coffin was lowered without any religious service. Notwithstanding Hatfield's various and complicated enormities, his untimely end excited considerable commiseration. His manners were extremely polished and insinuating, and he was possessed of qualities which might have rendered him an ornament to society.

The unfortunate Mary of Buttermere went from home to avoid the impertinent visits of unfeeling curiosity. She was much affected; and, indeed, without supposing that any part of her former attachment remained, it is impossible that she could view his tragical fate with indifference. When her father and mother heard that Hatfield had certainly been hanged, they both exclaimed, 'God be thanked!'

On the day of his condemnation, Wordsworth and Coleridge passed through Carlisle, and endeavoured to obtain an interview with him. Wordsworth succeeded; but, for some unknown reason, the prisoner steadily refused to see Coleridge; a caprice which could not be penetrated. It was true that he had, during his whole residence at Keswick, avoided Coleridge with a solicitude which had revived the original suspicions against him in some quarters, after they had generally subsided. However, if not him, Coleridge saw and examined his very interesting papers. These were chiefly letters from women whom he had injured, pretty much in the same way, and by the same impostures, as he had recently practised in Cumberland. Great was the emotion of Coleridge when he afterwards recurred to these letters, and bitter—almost vindictive—was the indignation with which he spoke of Hatfield. One set of letters appeared to have been written under too certain a knowledge of his villainy towards the individual to whom they were addressed; though still relying on some possible remains of humanity, or perhaps (the poor writer might think) on some lingering relics of affection for herself.

The other set was even more distressing; they were written under the first conflicts of suspicions, alternately repelling with warmth the gloomy doubts which were fast arising, and then yielding to their afflicting evidence; raving in one page under the misery of alarm, in another courting the delusions of hope, and luring back the perfidious deserter—here resigning herself to despair, and there again labouring to show that all might yet be well. Coleridge said often, in looking back upon that frightful exposure of human guilt and misery, that the man who, when pursued by these heart-rending apostrophes, and with this litany of anguish sounding in his ears, from despairing women, and from famishing children, could yet find it possible to enjoy the calm pleasures of a lake tourist, and deliberately to hunt for the picturesque, must have been a fiend of that order which, fortunately, does not often emerge amongst men.

It is painful to remember that, in those days, amongst the multitudes who ended their career in the same ignominious

way, and the majority for offences connected with the
forgery of bank notes, there must have been a considerable
number who perished from the very opposite cause; namely,
because they felt, too passionately and profoundly for pru-
dence, the claims of those who looked up to them for support. One common scaffold confounds the most flinty hearts
and the tenderest. However, in this instance, it was in some
measure the heartless part of Hatfield's conduct which drew
upon him his ruin; for the Cumberland jury, it has been
asserted, declared their unwillingness to hang him for having
forged a frank; and both they, and those who refused to aid
his escape, when first apprehended, were reconciled to this
harshness entirely by what they had heard of his conduct
to their injured young fellow-countrywoman.

She, meantime, under the name of the Beauty of Buttermere, became an object of interest to all England. Dramas
and melo-dramas were produced in the London theatres
upon her story; and for many a year afterwards, shoals of
tourists crowded to the secluded lake and the little homely
cabaret, which had been the scene of her brief romance. It
was fortunate for a person in her distressing situation, that
her home was not in a town; the few and simple who had
witnessed her imaginary elevation, having little knowledge
of worldly feelings, never for an instant connected with her
disappointment any sense of the ludicrous, or spoke of it as a
calamity to which her vanity might have co-operated. They
treated it as unmixed injury, reflecting shame upon nobody
but the wicked perpetrator. Hence, without much trial to her
womanly sensibilities, she found herself able to resume her
situation in the little inn; and this she continued to hold for
many years. In that place, and in that capacity, she was seen
repeatedly. She was greatly admired, and became the subject
of the poet's song; but 'sorrow,' to use the beautiful language
of Ossian, 'sorrow, like a cloud on the sun, shaded her soul.'

Broad Stand

3

Trance
and
Delight

SAMUEL
TAYLOR
COLERIDGE

*Defoe found the place 'monstrous'; fifty years later Gilpin found
it 'picturesque'; thirty years after that Coleridge was scrambling
all over it with the zest of Chris Bonington. In fact, it is amazing
that in this small area so many different and difficult climbs can
be encountered that it is now considered a useful place to train for
some of the highest peaks in Nepal. There was a time, at the end
of the last century, when rock-climbing, scholarship, Englishness
and love of the place itself first co-existed in an exceptional
harmony which has come to be a local tradition. I was sorry that
there wasn't room to include an extract from the writings of Owen
Glynne Jones, member of the Alpine Club, and perhaps the most
typical example of that harmony. But here, at least, is Samuel
Taylor Coleridge, writing to Sara Hutchinson, whom he loved but
whom he was not free to marry. With a mighty intellect and an
enlarged heart, a sad wife and an addiction to opium, a widely
held place of honour as a conversationalist without equal, and an
intense manic depressive degree of self-loathing, Coleridge became
the first rock-climber to go into print; and this is how the climb
happened, a hundred and eighty years ago.*

ESKDALE, FRIDAY, AUGT. 6th. 1802
AT AN ESTATE HOUSE CALLED TOES

There is one sort of Gambling, to which I am much

addicted; and that not of the least criminal kind for a man who has children & a Concern.—It is this. When I find it convenient to descend from a mountain, I am too confident & too indolent to look round about & wind about 'till I find a track or other symptom of safety; but I wander on, & where it is first *possible* to descend, there I go—relying upon fortune for how far down this possibility will continue. So it was yesterday afternoon. I passed down from Broad-crag, skirted the Precipices, and found myself cut off from a most sublime Crag-summit, that seemed to rival Sca' Fell Man [see footnote, page 13] in height, & to outdo it in fierceness. A Ridge of Hill lay low down, & divided this Crag (called Doe-crag) & Broad-crag—even as the Hyphen divides the words broad & crag. I determined to go thither; the first place I came to, that was not direct Rock, I slipped down, & went on for a while with tolerable ease— but now I came (it was midway down) to a smooth perpendicular Rock about 7 feet high—this was nothing— I put my hands on the Ledge, & dropped down / in a few yards came just such another / *dropped* that too / and yet another, seemed not higher—I would not stand for a trifle / so I dropped that too / but the stretching of the muscle[s] of my hands & arms, & the jolt of the Fall on my Feet, put my whole Limbs in a *Tremble*, and I paused, & looking down, saw that I had little else to encounter but a succession of these little Precipices—it was in truth a Path that in a very hard Rain is, no doubt, the channel of a most splendid Waterfall.—So I began to suspect that I ought not to go on / but then unfortunately tho' I could with ease drop down a smooth Rock 7 feet high, I could not *climb* it / so go on I must / and on I went / the next 3 drops were not half a Foot, at least not a foot more than my own height / but every Drop increased the Palsy of my Limbs—I shook all over, Heaven knows without the least influence of Fear / and now I had only two more to drop down / to return was impossible—but of these two the first was tremendous / it was twice my own height, & the Ledge at the bottom was [so] exceedingly narrow, that if I dropt down upon it I must of necessity have fallen backwards & of course killed myself. My Limbs were all in a tremble—I lay upon my Back to rest myself, & was beginning according to my Custom to laugh

looking north

Scafell

Scafell Pikes

Great End

Esk House

Cam Spout

River Esk

Doin Sampson's Stones

Cat Crag

Heron Crag

River Esk

Taw House

at myself for a Madman, when the sight of the Crags above me on each side, & the impetuous Clouds just over them, posting so luridly & so rapidly northward, overawed me / I lay in a state of almost prophetic Trance & Delight—& blessed God aloud, for the powers of Reason & the Will, which remaining no Danger can overpower us! O God, I exclaimed aloud—how calm, how blessed am I now / I know not how to proceed, how to return / but I am calm & fearless & confident / if this Reality were a Dream, if I were asleep, what agonies had I suffered! what screams!—When the Reason & the Will are away, what remain to us but Darkness & Dimness & a bewildering Shame, and Pain that is utterly Lord over us, or fantastic Pleasure, that draws the Soul along swimming through the air in many shapes, even as a Flight of Starlings in a Wind.—I arose, & looking down saw at the bottom a heap of Stones— which had fallen abroad —and rendered the narrow Ledge on which they had been piled, doubly dangerous / at the bottom of the third Rock that I dropt from, I met a dead Sheep quite rotten—This heap of Stones, I guessed, & have since found that I guessed aright, had been piled up by the Shepherd to enable him to climb up & free the poor creature whom he had observed to be crag-fast—but seeing nothing but rock over rock, he had desisted & gone for help—& in the mean time the poor creature had fallen down & killed itself.—As I was looking at these I glanced my eye to my left, & observed that the Rock was rent from top to bottom—I measured the breadth of the Rent, and found that there was no danger of my being *wedged* in / so I put my Knap-sack round to my side, & slipped down as between two walls, without any danger or difficulty—the next Drop brought me down on the Ridge called the How / I hunted out my Besom Stick, which I had flung before me when I first came to the Rocks—and wisely gave over all thoughts of ascending Doe-Crag—for now the Clouds were again coming in most tumultuously— so I began to descend / when I felt an odd sensation across my whole Breast—not pain nor itching—& putting my hand on it I found it all bumpy—and on looking saw the whole of my Breast from my Neck [to my Navel]*—& exactly all that my Kamell-hair Breast-shield covers, filled with great red heat-bumps, so thick that no hair could lie between them. They still remain / but are evidently less—& I have no doubt will wholly disappear in a few Days. It was however a startling proof to me of the violent exertions which I had made. I descended this low Hill which was all hollow beneath me—and was like the rough green Quilt of a Bed of waters—at length two streams burst out & took their way down, one on [one] side a high Ground upon this Ridge, the other on the other—I took that to my right (having on my left this high Ground, & the other Stream, & beyond that Doe-crag, on the other side of which is Esk Halse, where the head-spring of the Esk rises, & running down the Hill & in upon the Vale looks and actually deceived me, as a great Turnpike Road—in which, as in many other respects the Head of Esk- dale much resembles Langdale) & soon the channel sank all at once, at least 40 yards, & formed a magnificent Waterfall— and close under this a succession of Waterfalls 7 in number, the third of which is nearly as high as the first. When I had almost reached the bottom of the Hill, I stood so as to com- mand the whole 8 Waterfalls, with the great triangle-Crag looking in above them, & on the one side of them the enor-

* Words in brackets inked out in the manuscript.

mous & more than perpendicular Precipices & *Bull's-Brows*,
of Sca' Fell! And now the Thunder-Storm was coming on,
again & again!—Just at the bottom of the Hill I saw on before
me in the Vale, lying just above the River on the side of a
Hill, one, two, three, four objects, I could not distinguish
whether Peat-hovels, or hovel-shaped Stones—I thought in
my mind, that 3 of them would turn out to be stones—but
that the fourth was certainly a Hovel. I went on toward them,
crossing & recrossing the Becks & the River & found that
they were all huge Stones—the one nearest the Beck which
I had determined to be really a Hovel, retained it's likeness
when I was close beside / in size it is nearly equal to the famous
Bowder stone, but in every other respect greatly superior to
it—it has a complete Roof, & that perfectly *thatched* with
weeds, & Heath, & Mountain-Ash Bushes—I now was
obliged to ascend again, as the River ran greatly to the Left,
& the Vale was nothing more than the Channel of the River,
all the rest of the interspace between the mountains was a
tossing up & down of Hills of all sizes—and the place at which
I am now writing is called—*Te-as*, & spelt, *Toes*—as the Toes
of Sca' Fell—. It is not possible that any name can be more
descriptive of the Head of Eskdale—I ascended close under
Sca' Fell, & came to a little Village of Sheep-folds / there
were 5 together / & the redding Stuff, & the Shears, & an
old Pot, was in the Passage of the first of them. Here I found
an imperfect Shelter from a Thunder-shower—accompanied
with such Echoes! O God! what thoughts were mine! O how
I wished for Health & Strength that I might wander about
for a Month together, in the stormiest month of the year,
among these Places, so lonely & savage & full of sounds!

  *After the Thunder-storm I shouted out all your names
in the Sheep-fold—when Echo came upon Echo / and then
Hartley & Derwent [his sons] & then I laughed & shouted
Joanna [*cf* Wordsworth's poem, *To Joanna*] / It leaves all the
Echoes I ever heard far far behind, in number, distinctness &
humanness of Voice—& then not to forget an old Friend I
made them all say Dr Dodd &c.—

---

* This paragraph, which forms the conclusion of the letter in the
  Sara Hutchinson journal, has been transferred here to keep the
  events of the tour chronological.

After the Storm I passed on & came to a great Peat-road, that wound down a hill, called Maddock How, & now came out upon the first cultivated Land which begins with a Bridge that goes over a Stream, a Waterfall of considerable height & beautifully wooded above you, & a great waterslope under you / the Gill down which it falls, is called Scale Gill—and the Fall Scale Gill Force. (The word Scale & Scales is common in this Country—& is said by ... [name omitted] to be derived from the Saxon Sceala; the wattling of Sheep—but judging from the places themselves, *Scale Force* & this Scale Gill Force—I think it is as probable that it is derived from Scalle—which signifies a deafening Noise.) Well, I passed thro' some sweet pretty Fields, & came to a large Farmhouse where I am now writing / The place is called Toes or *Te* as—the master's name John Vicars Towers—they received me hospitably / I drank Tea here & they begged me to pass the Night—which I did & supped of some excellent Salmonlings, which Towers had brought from Ravenglass whither he had been, as holding under the Earl of Egremont, & obliged 'to ride the Fair'—a custom introduced during the times of Insecurity & piratical Incursion for the Protection of Ravenglass Fair. They were a fine Family—and a Girl who did not look more than 12 years old, but was nearly 15, was very beautiful—with hair like vine-tendrils—. She had been long ill—& was a sickly child—'Ah poor Bairn! (said the Mother) worse luck for her / she looks like a Quality Bairn, as you may say.' This man's Ancestors have been time out of mind in the Vale / and here I found that the common Names, Towers, & Tozers are the same— / *er* signifies 'upon' —as Mite-er-dale the Dale upon the River Mite / Donnerdale—a contraction of Duddon-er-dale the Dale upon the River Duddon—So Towers, pronounced in the Vale *Te*-ars —& Tozers is those who live on *the Toes*—i.e. upon the *Knobby* feet of the Mountain / Mr *Tears* has mended my pen.—This morning after breakfast I went out with him, & passed up the Vale again due East, along a higher Road, over a heathy upland, crossed the upper part of Scale Gill, came out upon Maddock How, & then ascending turned directly Northward, into the Heart of the mountains; on my left the wild Crags under which flows the Scale Gill Beck, the most remarkable of them called Cat Crag (a wild Cat being killed there) & on my right hand six great Crags, which appeared in the mist all in a file—and they were all, tho' of different sizes, yet the same shape all triangles—. Other Crags far above them, higher up the Vale, appeared & disappeared as the mists passed & came / one with a waterfall, called Spout Crag—and another most tremendous one, called Earn [Heron] Crag—I passed on, a little way, till I came close under a huge Crag, called Buck Crag—& immediately under this is Four-foot Stone—having on it the clear marks of four foot-steps. The Stone is in it's whole breadth just 36 inches, (I measured it exactly) but the part that contains the marks is raised above the other part, & is just 20½ Inches. The length of the Stone is 32½ Inches. The first foot-mark is an Ox's foot—nothing can be conceived more exact—this is 5¾ Inches wide—the second is a Boy's shoe in the Snow, 9½ Inches in length / this too is the very Thing itself, the Heel, the bend of the Foot, &c.—the third is the Foot-step to the very Life of a Mastiff Dog—and the fourth *is Derwent's very own first little Shoe*, 4 Inches in length & O! it is the sweetest Baby shoe that ever was seen.—The wie-foot in Borrowdale is contemptible; but this really does work upon my imagination very powerfully / & I will try to construct a Tale upon it / the place too is so very, very wild. I delighted the Shepherd by my admiration / & the four foot Stone is my own Christening, & Towers undertakes it shall hereafter go by that name for hitherto it has been nameless.—And so I returned & have found a Pedlar here of an interesting Physiognomy—& here I must leave off—for Dinner is ready—

On August 10, after his return to Keswick, Coleridge wrote to Sara saying that he had not yet finished this 'Great-sheet' letter; probably he never did so.

4

The Wilds of Carrock

CHARLES DICKENS

In its full flood of fashion, no literary man could afford not to have been seen on a fell. Charles Dickens' description of his adventures in the Northern Fells is simply the best prose written about the place. It is a hymn to all fell-failures by a man whose genius gained its deserved success. Except on Carrock.

★   ★   ★

In the month of September, 1857, two idle London apprentices, exhausted by the long, hot summer, and the long, hot work it had brought with it, ran away from their employer. Mr Thomas Idle and Mr Francis Goodchild took the train to Carlisle and thence, at eight o'clock one forenoon, they rode out to the village of Hesket Newmarket, some 14 miles distant.

Goodchild (who had already begun to doubt whether he was idle: as his way always is when he has nothing to do) had read of a certain black old Cumberland hill or mountain, called Carrock, or Carrock Fell; and had arrived at the conclusion that it would be the culminating triumph of Idleness to ascend the same. Thomas Idle, dwelling on the pains inseparable from that achievement, had expressed the strongest doubts of the expediency, and even of the sanity, of the enterprise; but Goodchild had carried his point, and they rode away.

Up hill and down hill, and twisting to the right, and twisting to the left, and with old Skiddaw (who has vaunted himself a great deal more than his merits deserve; but that is rather the way of the Lake country), dodging the apprentices in a picturesque and pleasant manner. Good, weather-proof, warm, pleasant houses, well white-limed, scantily dotting the road. Clean children coming out to look, carrying other clean children as big as themselves. Harvest still lying out and much rained upon; here and there, harvest still unreaped. Well-cultivated gardens attached to the cottages, with plenty of produce forced out of their hard soil. Lonely nooks, and wild; but people can be born, and married, and buried in such nooks, and can live and love, and be loved, there as elsewhere, thank God! (Mr Goodchild's remark.) By-and-by, the village. Black, coarse-stoned, rough-windowed houses; some with outer staircases, like Swiss houses; a sinuous and stony gutter winding up hill and round the corner, by way of the street. All the children running out directly. Women pausing in washing, to peep from doorways and very little windows. Such were the observations of Messrs Idle and Goodchild, as their conveyance stopped at the village shoemaker's. Old Carrock gloomed down upon it all in a very ill-tempered state; and the rain was beginning.

The village shoemaker declined to have anything to do with Carrock. No visitors went up Carrock. No visitors came there at all. Aa' the world ganged awa' yon. The driver appealed to the Innkeeper. The Innkeeper had two men working in the fields, and one of them should be called in, to go up Carrock as guide. Messrs Idle and Goodchild, highly approving, entered the Innkeeper's house, to drink whiskey and eat oatcake.

The Innkeeper was not idle enough—was not idle at all, which was a great fault in him—but was a fine specimen of a north-countryman, or any kind of man. He had a ruddy cheek, a bright eye, a well-knit frame, an immense hand, a cheery outspeaking voice, and a straight, bright, broad look. He had a drawing-room, too, upstairs which was worth a visit to the Cumberland Fells. (This was Mr Francis Goodchild's opinion, in which Mr Thomas Idle did not concur.)

The two apprentices settled happily in the drawing-room, which was comfortably and solidly furnished with good mahogany and horsehair. It had a snug fireside, and a couple of well-curtained windows, looking out upon the wild country behind the house, and was crammed with little ornaments.

Mr Idle and Mr Goodchild never asked themselves how it came to pass that the men in the fields were never heard of more, how the stalwart landlord replaced them without explanation, how his dog-cart came to be waiting at the door, and how everything was arranged without the least arrangement for climbing to old Carrock's shoulders, and standing on his head.

Without a word of inquiry, therefore, the Two Idle Apprentices drifted out resignedly into a fine, soft, close, drowsy, penetrating rain; got into the landlord's light dog-cart, and rattled off through the village for the foot of Carrock. The journey at the outset was not remarkable. The Cumberland road went up and down like all other roads; the Cumberland curs burst out from backs of cottages and barked like other curs, and the Cumberland peasantry stared after the dog-cart amazedly, as long as it was in sight, like the rest of their race. The approach to the foot of the mountain resembled the approaches to the feet of most other mountains all over the world. The cultivation gradually ceased, the trees grew gradually rare, the road became gradually rougher, and the sides of the mountain looked gradually more and more lofty, and more and more difficult to get up. The dog-cart was left at a lonely farm-house. The landlord borrowed a large umbrella, and, assuming in an instant the character of the most cheerful and adventurous of guides, led the way to the ascent. Mr Goodchild looked eagerly at the top of the mountain, and, feeling apparently that he was now going to be very lazy indeed, shone all over wonderfully to the eye, under the influence of the contentment within and the moisture without. Only in the bosom of Mr Thomas Idle did Despondency now hold her gloomy state. He kept it a secret; but he would have given a very handsome sum, when the ascent began, to have been back again at the inn. The sides of Carrock looked fearfully steep, and the top of Carrock was hidden in mist. The rain was falling faster and faster. The knees of Mr Idle—always weak on walking excursions—shivered and shook with fear and damp. The wet was already penetrating through the young man's outer coat to a brand-new shooting-jacket, for which he had reluctantly paid the large sum of two guineas on leaving town; he had no stimulating refreshment about him but a small packet of clammy gingerbread nuts; he had nobody to give him an arm, nobody to push him gently behind, nobody to pull him up tenderly in front, nobody to speak to who really felt the difficulties of the ascent, the dampness of the rain, the denseness of the mist, and the unutterable folly of climbing, undriven, up any steep place in the world, when there is level ground within reach to walk on instead. Was it for this that Thomas had left London? London, where there are nice short walks in level public gardens, with benches of repose set up at convenient distances for weary travellers—London, where rugged stone is humanely pounded into little lumps for the road, and intelligently shaped into smooth slabs for the pavement! No! it was not for the laborious ascent of the crags of Carrock that Idle had left his native city, and travelled to Cumberland. Never did he feel more disastrously convinced that he had committed a very grave error in judgment than when he found himself standing in the rain at the bottom of a steep mountain, and knew that the responsibility rested on his weak shoulders of actually getting to the top of it.

The honest landlord went first, the beaming Goodchild followed, the mournful Idle brought up the rear. From time to time, the two foremost members of the expedition changed places in the order of march; but the rearguard never altered his position. Up the mountain or down the mountain, in the water or out of it, over the rocks, through the bogs, skirting the heather, Mr Thomas Idle was always the last, and was always the man who had to be looked after and waited for. At first the ascent was delusively easy, the sides of the mountain sloped gradually, and the material of which they were composed was a soft, spongy turf, very tender and pleasant to walk upon. After a hundred yards or so, however, the verdant scene and the easy slope disappeared, and the rocks began. Not noble, massive rocks, standing upright, keeping a certain regularity in their positions, and possessing, now and then, flat tops to sit upon, but little irritating, comfortless rocks, littered about anyhow by Nature; treacherous, disheartening rocks of all sorts of small shapes and small sizes, bruisers of tender toes and trippers-up of wavering feet. When these impediments were passed, heather and slough followed. Here the steepness of the ascent was slightly mitigated; and here the exploring party of three turned round to look at the view below them. The scene of the moorland and the fields was like a feeble water-colour drawing half sponged out. The mist was darkening, the rain was thickening, the trees were dotted about like spots of faint shadow, the division-lines which mapped out the fields were all getting blurred together, and the lonely farm-house where the dog-cart had been left, loomed spectral in the grey light like the last human dwelling at the end of the habitable world. Was this a sight worth climbing to see? Surely—surely not!

Up again—for the top of Carrock is not reached yet. The landlord, just as good-tempered and obliging as he was at the bottom of the mountain. Mr Goodchild brighter in the eyes and rosier in the face than ever; full of cheerful remarks and apt quotations, and walking with a springiness of step wonderful to behold. Mr Idle, farther and farther in the rear, with the water squeaking in the toes of his boots, with his two-guinea shooting jacket clinging damply to his aching sides, with his overcoat so full of rain, and standing out so pyramidically stiff, in consequence, from his shoulders downwards, that he felt as if he was walking in a gigantic ex-tinguisher—the despairing spirit within him representing but too aptly the candle that had just been put out. Up and up and up again, till a ridge is reached and the outer edge of the mist on the summit of Carrock is darkly and drizzlingly near. Is this the top? No, nothing like the top. It is an aggravat-ing peculiarity of all mountains that, although they have only one top when they are seen (as they ought always to be seen) from below, they turn out to have a perfect eruption of false tops whenever the traveller is sufficiently ill-advised to go out of his way for the purpose of ascending them. Carrock is but a trumpery little mountain of fifteen hundred feet, and it pre-sumes to have false tops, and even precipices, as if it were Mont Blanc. No matter; Goodchild enjoys it, and will go on; and Idle, who is afraid of being left behind by himself, must follow. On entering the edge of the mist, the landlord stops, and says he hopes that it will not get any thicker. It is twenty years since he last ascended Carrock, and it is barely possible, if the mist increases, that the party may be lost on the mountain. Goodchild hears this dreadful intimation, and is not in the least impressed by it. He marches for the top that is never to be found, as if he was the Wandering Jew, bound to go on for ever, in defiance of everything. The landlord faithfully accompanies him. The two, to the dim eye of Idle, far below, look in the exaggerative mist, like a pair of friendly giants, mounting the steps of some invisible castle together. Up and up, and then down a little, and then up, and then along a strip of level ground, and then up again. The wind, a wind unknown in the happy valley, blows keen and strong; the rain-mist gets impenetrable; a dreary little cairn of stones appears. The landlord adds one to the heap, first walking all round the cairn as if he were about to perform an incantation, then dropping the stone on to the top of the heap with the gesture of a magician adding an ingredient to a cauldron in full bubble. Goodchild sits down by the cairn as if it were his study-table at home; Idle, drenched and panting, stands up with his back to the wind, ascertains distinctly that this is the top at last, looks round with all the little curiosity that is left in him, and gets in return, a magnificent view of—Nothing!

The effect of this sublime spectacle on the minds of the exploring party is a little injured by the nature of the direct conclusion to which the sight of it points—the said conclusion being that the mountain mist has actually gathered round them, as the landlord feared it would. It now becomes imperatively necessary to settle the exact situation of the farm-house in the valley at which the dog-cart has been left, before the travellers attempt to descend. While the landlord is endeavouring to make this discovery in his own way, Mr Goodchild plunges his hand under his wet coat, draws out a little red morocco-case, opens it, and displays to the view of his companions a neat pocket-compass. The north is found, the point at which the farm-house is situated is settled, and the descent begins. After a little downward walking, Idle (behind as usual) sees his fellow-travellers turn aside sharply—tries to follow them—loses them in the mist—is shouted after, waited for, recovered—and then finds that a halt has been ordered, partly on his account, partly for the purpose of again consulting the compass.

The point in debate is settled as before between Goodchild and the landlord, and the expedition moves on, not down the mountain, but marching straight forward round the slope of it. The difficulty of following this new route is acutely felt by Thomas Idle. He finds the hardship of walking at all greatly increased by the fatigue of moving his feet straight forward along the side of a slope, when their natural tendency, at every step, is to turn off at a right angle, and go straight down the declivity. Let the reader imagine himself to be walking along the roof of a barn, instead of up or down it, and he will have an exact idea of the pedestrian difficulty in which the travellers had now involved themselves. In ten minutes more Idle was lost in the distance again, was shouted for, waited for, recovered as before; found Goodchild repeating his observation of the compass, and remonstrated warmly against the sideway route that his companions persisted in following. It appeared to the uninstructed mind of Thomas that when three men want to get to the bottom of a mountain, their business is to walk down it; and he put this view of the case, not only with emphasis, but even with some irritability. He was answered from the scientific eminence of the compass on which his companions were mounted, that there was a frightful chasm somewhere near the foot of Carrock, called The Black Arches, into which the travellers were sure to march in the mist, if they risked continuing the descent from the place where they had now halted. Idle received this answer with the silent respect which was due to the commanders of the expedition, and followed along the roof of the barn, or rather the side of the mountain, reflecting upon the assurance which he had received on starting again, that the object of the party was only to gain 'a certain point,' and, this haven attained, to continue the descent afterwards until the foot of Carrock was reached. Though quite unexceptionable as an abstract form of expression, the phrase 'a certain point' has the disadvantage of sounding rather vaguely when it is pronounced on unknown ground, under a canopy of mist much thicker than a London fog. Nevertheless, after the compass, this phrase was all the clue the party had to hold by, and Idle clung to the extreme end of it as hopefully as he could.

More sideway walking, thicker and thicker mist, all sorts

of points reached except the 'certain point'; third loss of Idle, third shouts for him, third recovery of him, third consultation of compass. Mr Goodchild draws it tenderly from his pocket, and prepares to adjust it on a stone. Something falls on the turf—it is the glass. Something else drops immediately after—it is the needle. The compass is broken, and the exploring party is lost!

It is the practice of the English portion of the human race to receive all great disasters in dead silence. Mr Goodchild restored the useless compass to his pocket without saying a word. Mr Idle looked at the landlord, and the landlord looked at Mr Idle. There was nothing for it now but to go on blindfold, and trust to the chapter of chances. Accordingly, the lost travellers moved forward, still walking round the slope of the mountain, still desperately resolved to avoid the Black Arches, and to succeed in reaching the 'certain point'.

A quarter of an hour brought them to the brink of a ravine, at the bottom of which there flowed a muddy little stream. Here another halt was called, and another consultation took place. The landlord, still clinging pertinaciously to the idea of reaching the 'point', voted for crossing the ravine, and going on round the slope of the mountain. Mr Goodchild, to the great relief of his fellow-traveller, took another view of the case, and backed Mr Idle's proposal to descend Carrock at once, at any hazard—the rather as the running stream was a sure guide to follow from the mountain to the valley. Accordingly, the party descended to the rugged and stony banks of the stream; and here again Thomas lost ground sadly, and fell far behind his travelling companions. Not much more than six weeks had elapsed since he had sprained one of his ankles, and he began to feel this same ankle getting rather weak when he found himself among the stones that were strewn about the running water. Goodchild and the landlord were getting farther and farther ahead of him. He saw them cross the stream and disappear round a projection on its banks. He heard them shout the moment after as a signal that they had halted and were waiting for him. Answering the shout, he mended his pace, crossed the stream where they had crossed it, and was within one step of the opposite bank, when his foot slipped on a wet stone, his weak ankle gave a twist outwards, a hot, rending, tearing pain ran through it at the same moment, and down fell the idlest of the Two Idle Apprentices, crippled in an instant.

The situation was now, in plain terms, one of absolute danger. There lay Mr Idle writhing in pain, there was the mist as thick as ever, there was the landlord as completely lost as the strangers whom he was conducting, and there was the compass broken in Goodchild's pocket. To leave the wretched Thomas on unknown ground was plainly impossible, and to get him to walk with a badly sprained ankle seemed equally out of the question. However, Goodchild (brought back by his cry for help) bandaged the ankle with a pocket-handkerchief, and assisted by the landlord, raised the crippled Apprentice to his legs, offered him a shoulder to lean on, and exhorted him for the sake of the whole party to try if he could walk. Thomas, assisted by the shoulder on the one side, and a stick on the other, did try, with what pain and difficulty those only can imagine who have sprained an ankle and have had to tread on it afterwards. At a pace adapted to the feeble hobbling of a newly-lamed man, the lost party moved on, perfectly ignorant whether they were on the right side of the mountain or the wrong, and equally uncertain how long Idle would be able to contend with the pain in his ankle, before he gave in altogether and fell down again, unable to stir another step.

Slowly and more slowly, as the clog of crippled Thomas weighed heavily and more heavily on the march of the expedition, the lost travellers followed the windings of the stream, till they came to a faintly marked cart-track, branching off nearly at right angles, to the left. After a little consultation it was resolved to follow this dim vestige of a road in the hope that it might lead to a farm or cottage, at which Idle could be left in safety. It was now getting on towards the afternoon, and it was fast becoming more than doubtful whether the party, delayed in their progress as they now were, might not be overtaken by the darkness before the right route was found, and be condemned to pass the night on the mountain, without bite or drop to comfort them, in their wet clothes.

The cart-track grew fainter and fainter, until it was washed out altogether by another little stream, dark, turbulent, and rapid. The landlord suggested, judging by the colour of the water, that it must be flowing from one of the lead mines in the neighbourhood of Carrock; and the travellers accordingly kept by the stream for a little while, in the hope of possibly wandering towards help in that way. After walking forward about two hundred yards, they came upon a mine indeed, but a mine exhausted and abandoned; a dismal, ruinous place, with nothing but the wreck of its works and buildings left to speak for it. Here, there were a few sheep feeding. The landlord looked at them earnestly, thought he recognised the marks on them—then thought he did not—finally gave up the sheep in despair—and walked on just as ignorant of the whereabouts of the party as ever.

The march in the dark, literally as well as metaphorically in the dark, had now been continued for three-quarters of an hour from the time when the crippled Apprentice had met with his accident. Mr Idle, with all the will to conquer the pain in his ankle, and to hobble on, found the power rapidly failing him, and felt that another ten minutes at most would find him at the end of his last physical resources. He had just made up his mind on this point, and was about to communicate the dismal result of his reflections to his companions, when the mist suddenly brightened, and begun to lift straight ahead. In another minute, the landlord, who was in advance, proclaimed that he saw a tree. Before long, other trees appeared—then a cottage—then a house beyond the cottage, and a familiar line of road rising behind it. Last of all, Carrock itself loomed darkly into view, far away to the right hand. The party had not only got down the mountain without knowing how, but had wandered away from it in the mist, without knowing why—away, far down on the very moor by which they had approached the base of Carrock that morning.

The happy lifting of the mist, and the still happier discovery that the travellers had groped their way, though by a very roundabout direction, to within a mile or so of the part of the valley in which the farm-house was situated, restored Mr Idle's sinking spirits and reanimated his failing strength. While the landlord ran off to get the dog-cart, Thomas was assisted by Goodchild to the cottage which had been the first building seen when the darkness brightened, and was propped up against the garden wall, like an artist's lay figure waiting to be forwarded, until the dog-cart should arrive from the farm-house below. In due time—and a very long time it seemed to Mr Idle—the rattle of wheels was heard, and the crippled Apprentice was lifted into the seat. As the dog-cart was driven back to the inn, the landlord related an anecdote which he had just heard at the farm-house, of an unhappy man who had been lost, like his two guests and himself, on Carrock; who had passed the night there alone; who had been found the next morning, 'scared and starved'; and who never went out afterwards, except on his way to the grave. Mr Idle heard this sad story, and derived at least one useful impression from it. Bad as the pain in his ankle was, he contrived to bear it patiently, for he felt grateful that a worse accident had not befallen him in the wilds of Carrock.

5

Windermere 1895

BEATRIX POTTER

Peter Rabbit is possibly as widely known a character as Oliver Twist. He was invented by Beatrix Potter around Windermere. For a while I thought of including one of her stories but in the end I have selected a few pages from her journals. These were discovered in code writing. Leslie Linder did this transcription. What the journals show (rather like the journals of Dorothy Wordsworth) is the continuous and intent concern with what was happening on the writer's own patch. There is a curiosity about the everyday which is both moving and impressive. These quiet days in what was such an isolated spot now seem so full that we envy the limitations which bred them.

Friday, July 26th [1895]. July 26th we came to Holehird, Windermere, where we tarried in the summer of 89 when I could hardly walk at all, for which be thankful. I am very much struck with the difference. I had never been on the hill behind the house, only once in the copse.

We found the pleasant old gardener dead and gone, and a bustling self-important personage in his place, who amused me but exasperated Bertram [her brother] by giving him permission to pick raspberries. Mr Anthony Wilkinson ('by gum its währm'), very much alive, ('I—los—my second in —a—con—finement!') also one of the same carriage-horses, the worse for wear. We had rather wet weather, arriving on the heels of a thunderstorm.

Wednesday, July 31st. Went to Wray Castle July 31st., delighted to see old Foxcroft and Jane. The old man eighty-three, not a bit deaf, and funnier than ever, sitting in the sun in carpet-slippers. The house topsy-turvy after the tenancy of Mr Lumm who had left it, 'its filthy'....

I had some good luck finding funguses in the rain.

Aunt Clara and Miss Gentile arrived, and the weather was atrocious. Aunt Clara heavy and out of spirits, Miss Gentile odious.

Wednesday, August 7th. My first great day of fossils Aug. 7th when I drove up Troutbeck, overtaking a young farmer with a string of horses. Left the pony in the road and walked up Nanny Lane leading to the foot path up Wansfell. I had to go high, nearly level with the quarries across the valley before I came to a part where the walls were crumbling stone.

I found many shells, and when I had turned to come down, spied something sticking up grey on the top of a wall. I took it for a sheep's horn till I had it in my hand. It is a very steep, wide lane between high walls, a wonderful view. I could see the glint of a window or glass across Lancaster Sands.

Thursday, August 8th. Drove with aunt Clara and Miss Gentile to Coniston and back by Tilberthwaite. Miss Gentile has as much sentiment as a broom-stick, and appeared principally interested by the *sit*-uation of the Hotels, Aunt Clara half asleep. The only place where she showed any animation was the turn of the valley towards Holme Ground.

There is a great wreckage of fir trees in the gap at the top of the hill above the Marshalls, down which we came faster than I approved. I seemed to remember every bush on the road, and through the opera glass, on the hill-side above Coniston Bank. Not that five years is long, but I had so much forgotten this in six. I think I must have been in very weak health when I was here before, though not conscious of it to complaining at the time.

I was very much struck with the ideal beauty of Coniston. It was a perfect day, but apart from weather it is in my opinion far the most beautiful of the larger Lakes. Esthwaite and Blelham being reckoned with the small. It is so compact and the ground and vegetation so varied. Close down to the Lake the wild flowers were lovely.

I parted with aunt Clara and the interminable Miss Gentile and posted along the dusty road in the hot sun, looked at the exact spot in the roadside where Billy Hamilton, the blind

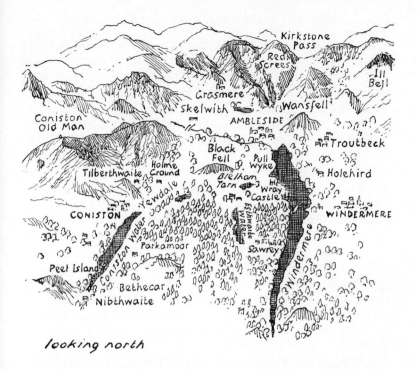

looking north

man used to stand, also I heard in the Village that the good-tempered, amiable creature was dead, two years since.

Blind men are reputed to be Saints, but they are generally sour. Billy must have absorbed the baking sunshine through his pores as he stood in the ditch. He came boldly up to the pony-carriage holding his hands like a scoop, and never failed to thank 'Mr Potter' by name, with broad grins. He also went about with a wheel-barrow collecting sticks, entering thickets with the immunity of the men of Thessaly; he fulfilled the pious service of supplying chips for the stove in Coniston Church.

I had a long talk with the postmistress, a lame girl on crutches. I went afterwards to see Miss Hanes in an old row of cottages above the Sky Hill—a little, thin, elderly woman with black hair and eyes, in spectacles, with a clean cottage and soapy hands.

I heard a long history of her daughter Jane, a girl to whom we took a great fancy, which seems to have been mutual unless butter entered into our conversation. I heard the history of Jane not marrying a coachman who took to drinking, and lost his place after the banns were put up; but the queer part of it was the way the course of events was taken, not as a disappointment but as a positive success, in the very nick of time, and he had turned out so very badly since.

Then I turned to cats, caäts, a he 'cart', a black Persian named Sādi whom we had bestowed on Jane. I should fail to give an impression of old Mrs Hanes looking over her spectacles and gesticulating in the middle of the flagged kitchen, nor would the joke be perceived without previous knowledge of Sādi, whom I saw last as a splendid half-grown kitten of diabolical temperament. 'He wad stand on the table and clar ye', she thought the world of that caät. Also he was 'moross' which I can well believe from what I saw of him.

When they took him to Liverpool he led them a dance, Jane wad be up ladders and over walls. Mrs Goodison thought the world of that caät. Mr Goodison didn't. It used to go to sleep in his arm chair and he was afraid to stir it. It was a trojan. It died of a consumption when it was only three.

I walked after lunch as far as Tent Lodge, and much regretted I could not go on to Coniston Bank to see Barnes and especially Mrs Barnes, a fine old Cumberland farmer's wife, homely and comely. We drove home by Yewdale and Skelwith.

Saturday, August 10th. In afternoon went with the pony up Troutbeck and put it up at the Mortal Man which looks a very nice little inn. Papa and I walked up Nanny Lane and got over a stile into the heather, sweet and heavy with honey. There was a thunder-haze, no view, but very peaceful, except that the stone walls were covered with flying-ants.

I did not find many fossils, but we had great pleasure watching a pair of buzzards sailing round and round over the top of Wansfell. There was an old shepherd half way up the side of Troutbeck, much bent and gesticulating with a stick. He watched the collie scouring round over stone walls, coming close past us without taking the slightest notice. Four or five sheep louped over a wall at least three feet high on our right and escaped the dog's observation, whereupon the ancient shepherd, a mere speck in the slanting sunlight down the great hillside, this aged Wordsworthian worthy, awoke the echoes with a flood of the most singularly bad language. He gesticulated and the dog ran round on the top of dykes, and some young cattle ran down with their tails in the air.

It is most curious how sound travels up either side of the steep Troutbeck valley, but in keeping to be greeted with the classical but not time-honoured phrase addressed by La Pucelle to invaders. We passed him sitting on a wall as we came down, a pleasant, smiling old fellow. We asked him which was Ill Bell and he leant over the wall, 'ye'll perceive I'm rather hard of hearing', then heard that the prize-pup at Kelso Show was named 'Sandy Walker'.

Tuesday, August 13th. 11.12 when aunt Clara left, and also the greater part of Tues. 13th. was very wet. The German Emperor was expected to pass on Tues. but did not, owing to weather. Many took the trouble to go down, but I, not being keen, put off to the eleventh hour, and a man came past on horseback taking word to Troutbeck.

I had a long, beautiful drive in the afternoon going up by Pull Wyke to the barn gates. Then I remembered a pleasant lane down to Skelwith Bridge, and the woman at the inn assured me that the *sharies* came that way. All I can say is that we met a gig half way down, and could not have passed it had not it on two wheels been next the bank.

It was very beautiful under Black Fell but I was rather nervous. I walked up to see the Force which was in deafening flood, one of these foolish lambs in the meadow below the bridge knee deep.

We consumed three whole hours waiting to see the Emperor, not very well worth it. I had seen him in London. I think he is stouter.

I was not particularly excited. I think it is disgraceful to drive fine horses like that. First came a messenger riding a good roan belonging to Bowness, which we could hear snorting before they came in sight, man and horse both dead-beat. He reported that the Emperor would be up in ten minutes, but it was twenty.

The procession consisted of a mounted policeman with a drawn sword in a state approaching apoplexy, the red coats of the Quorn Hunt, four or five of Lord Lonsdale's carriages, several hires, and spare horses straggling after them. There were two horses with an outside rider to each carriage, splendid chestnuts, thoroughbred, floundering along and clinking their shoes.

They were not going fast when we saw them, having come all the way from Patterdale without even stopping at Kirkstone to water the horses, to the indignation of mine host, and an assembly of three or four hundred who had reckoned on this act of mercy. I think His Majesty deserved an accident, and rather wonder he didn't have one considering the smallness of the little *Tiger* sitting on the box to work the brake.

The liveries were blue and yellow and the carriages much yellow, singularly ugly low tub, with leather top to shut up sideways. The Emperor, Lord Lonsdale and two ladies in the first, Lady Dudley etc. in the second.

There was a considerable crowd and very small flags, German ones bad to get at short notice, but plenty of tricolours. Lord Lonsdale is red-headed and has a harum-scarum reputation, but, according to Mr Edmonstone, less 'stupid' than his predecessor whom he had seen 'beastly droonk' in the road on a Sunday morning.

Thursday, August 15th. Went along to the Sour Howes quarry and found many fossils. Bertram left me and went on. I was a little afraid of the quarrymen but they made no remark. I could hear people talking and a deafening racket of a mower down below. After a time I began to slither and slide down the grass slope to Limefit Farm.

It is very curious coming down from overhead. I landed very wet in the farmyard and asked a farm-wench if I could get through to the high road, who referred me to 'Polly' who was taking lunch in a corner out of a mug, preparatory to mounting a gig drawn by a large cart-horse. She looked at me with great composure and said she thought so, presently adding with equal decision and a strong Lancashire tone, 'would I please leave the gate open'. She presently sortied in a brown cloak and a hat with two defiant feathers, reminding me comically of Sarah Andrew.

Friday, August 16th. Went in afternoon down the road, back through Storrs, got some funguses, rather hot and muggy.

Saturday, August 17th. Kirkstone in the coach with papa. Fetched back by carriage middle afternoon. Very pleasant, silent air on the hills, curious place. Began to have enough of it during afternoon. Three pairs of buzzards nesting un-

molested on Red Screes in one quarry. Innkeeper said he
could hear the young birds crying in the morning.

Coming down we stopped at the wonderful view over
Troutbeck Tongue, and blue shadows creeping up the head
of the den. The Troutbeck valley is exquisite when it is fine,
which is but seldom.

Sunday, August 18th. Went to the Troutbeck Chapel—Rev.
Parker. I wonder why Dissenting Ministers are so very un-
presentable. The congregation were quite clean and had their
hair cut. He preached a long text on the Angel appearing to
Manoah and his wife, better than I expected, though very
homely.

The Congregationalists are more liberal than the Meth-
odists and Baptists, and this shock-headed, earnest preacher
got forth a rational, amiable interpretation, finding sermons
in stones and heavenly messengers in every blessing,—yea
—even in those afflictions which at first sight appear to be
'emissaries of Satan'. I thought the singing very sweet, two
favourite hymns—*Oh early happy, lasting wish—We faintly
hear, we dully see, in differing phrase we pray*, and a young
woman behind me singing *Angels of the night* in a clear, firm
voice. Lancashire folks sing through their teeth so to speak.
I suppose very young, but quaintly earnest.

Monday, August 19th. To lunch with Edith.

Thursday, August 22nd. Grasmere Sports, marred by bad
accident at Waterhead which, however, we did not know of
till afterwards. Clouds of dust, threatening thunder, but no
rain. We went late and had difficulty in finding friends
among the crowd of carriages.

About nineteen dogs were thrown off, but two young
hounds turned back at once, puzzling about the meadow.
The spectators on the tarred wall received them with execra-
tions and shouts of 'any price agin yon doug!' Rattler won,
a lean, black-and-white hound from Ambleside. Five came
in running, a light-coloured dog named Barmaid leading
when they came in sight.

Rattler's victory appeared popular, Mr Wilkinson danced
on the box, slapping his thigh, and greeted the owner with
a flourish and a wink as we passed him at Rydal leading
home his two hounds. Indeed Mr Wilkinson raced so alarm-
ingly on his own account with a wagonette that we began

to wonder whether he was, to quote aunt Booth's expressive phrase, 'boozy', the lower-orders were so extensively, but the weather was some excuse.

Friday, August 23rd. There was a hound-trail and sheep dogs in Troutbeck which I did not know of in time. I had, however, a lovely drive in the afternoon to Blelham, curling and blue under the crisp, fresh breeze. The boggy ground was literally dry, and I waded through the sweet bog myrtle to look for the long-leaved sundew, which I remembered covering the black peat like a crimson carpet. I found it near Scanty, past the season.

I went along the Causeway to the projecting knoll of firs where I found *Boletus badius*. I did not venture far into Randy Pike Wood because I could see a drove of cattle through the trees, and memories of a bull, which caused me to dodge them.

Saturday, August 24th. Went to see Ginnet's Circus at Ambleside and had a good laugh. I would go any distance to see a Caravan (barring lion-taming), it is the only species of entertainment I care for.

Mr Ginnet himself hath gone-off in appearance since I saw him last on the same spot ten years since, when he rode a young red-roan bull. He has subsided into a most disastrous long frock-coat and long, tight trousers with about a foot of damp at the bottom of them, and cracked a whip feebly. Were I inclined to weave a romance I might suspect that he had had reverses not unconnected with the bottle.

The Circus has fallen-off in the way of horses which represent capital, and stronger in the variety line. Probably a boisterous element introduced by growing lads. The neat little jockey had developed into a big, loutish, rough rider, very gentle however with the little child Millie Ginnet. She was exceedingly pretty and nice-mannered in her clothes, and indeed seemed too well clothed under her bathing-drawers, a marvellous little bundle, by no means painfully proficient.

The scornful Madame Ansonia was arrayed in blue and silver, and, alighting from her piebald, put on goloshes publicly in the ring. The fair-haired enchantress did not appear unless indeed she had shrivelled into Madame Fontainebleau, who displayed her remarkable dogs in an anxious cockney accent, and twinkled about in high-heeled French boots and chilly apparel. Tights do not shock me in a tent associated with damp grass, they suggest nothing less prosaic than rheumatics and a painfully drudging life.

Most people are vagabonds, but the rain washes away part of their sin, and the constant change of audience is better than leering at the same idle youths night after night. But for ignoring her company (and half the scarves which she ought to jump), commend me to Madame Ansonia. She was a good looking young woman with dark hair and eyes.

The other madame (there were but two), displayed an old, very old iron-grey mare with a long, thin neck, and a long, thin tail which it swished in cadence with the music. I think it was the oldest horse I ever saw in a circus, and the best dancer, going through its piece with avidity just in front of the band, but so very, very old that I was apprehensive about its rising when it curtseyed.

The other horses were the piebald, a steady property-horse with a broad back, two creams, not by any means a pair, and two ponies, the smaller Joey very clever in the way of temper. The most amusing thing was a race between these two, which Joey won by cutting across the turf-ring to the immense delight of the school-children who composed three-quarters of the audience.

Then any gentleman whatever was invited to ride, which they did with bashful courage and no success, the ponies going down on their knees and tumbling them right and left.

There was a great sale of sweets and the occasional variety of streams of rain through the tent, and the opening of umbrellas. The circus-dogs who mingled freely with the audience were demoralised by a fox terrier on the stalls, otherwise a rickety erection covered with carpet. One bench of school-children was overturned by Joey.

The most skilful performers were two men on parallel bars, and Herr Wartenburg the Barrel-King, who climbed on to a high seat and, having wiped it with a pocket handkerchief, laid himself on his velveteen back with his heels in the air, and danced wrong side up to the tune of *The Keelrow* against a cylinder, and then an immense barrel, I suppose inflated with gas. He danced his feet most gracefully, in little pointed shoes.

The performing-dogs turned back-somersaults with agility, and one small poodle dressed in clown's jacket and trousers skipped energetically on its hind legs, two persons turning the rope. A stray dog appeared in the ring but was chivvied out.

The entrance to this scene of joy was through some yards of stone fall thrown down on a dunghill, which afforded a gentle slope to the meadow below.

I regret to tate that for the last week in August we had almost unceasing rain accompanied by storms of wind. I had plenty to do indoors, but our time is running out.

6

The Battle of Rannerdale

NICHOLAS SIZE

Many writers have been fascinated by the 'dark ages' of the Lakes. Did King Arthur really hold court in Carlisle? Did the venerable Bede come across from Northumbria? Did the Norsemen introduce ideas of republicanism which still held good around Hawkshead in Wordsworth's childhood? Above all, is the legend true that 'we'— the Britons and the Norsemen—were the only part of England not conquered by the invading Normans? It's agreeable to think so. In his novel The Secret Valley, *first published in 1930, and now re-issued by a Cumbrian bookseller, Nicholas Size describes a school-boy-stirring chapter in Lakeland 'history'. I would like it to have been like that.*

Nicholas Size kept the Fish Hotel at Buttermere. Walpole encouraged him to write and he produced three novels. He died at the age of eighty-six having negotiated fiercely with the local rural district council public health committee to be buried on the fells. His own epitaph reads:

> *No tombstone virtues will ornament my grave*
> *No over-confidence about salvation,*
> *Write me down one that loved his fellow men*
> *And was a credit to his generation.*

The grave overlooks 'The Secret Valley'.

The great camp at Papcastle was protected by the River Derwent, but the audacity of the enemy across the river was extraordinary. Desperate raids were constantly being made at one point or another, and a surprising number of men were killed.

Preparations were soon made for a crossing to the triangle of land where the River Cocker runs into the Derwent, near where Cockermouth Castle now stands. The customary Springtime drought had made the passage of the Derwent an easy matter, and very soon the new camp was fortified with stockades in spite of the frenzied attacks of the English.

Once the Normans were established, however, their enemies disappeared; the open and level country about Cockermouth was very favourable to the Normans, and they gradually made themselves masters of it, suffering, however, each night from persistent attacks designed to reduce their numbers.

The Norman armament was very superior to that of the English, and their mounted men, who bestrode the ancestors of our cart horses, seemed to be irresistible. Their pikemen and spearmen were well-disciplined and partly armoured, and their morale was excellent, for they knew they were being led towards a straightforward job which exactly suited them. No more were they expected to capture mountain ridges hidden in the mist, or to traverse ravines where there was hardly any foothold. No longer would each night's camping be a nightmare. They felt at last that their leaders knew what they were about, and without doubt quiet confidence pervaded all the army.

On the English side it had long been realised that the final chapter of the struggle was very near, and to many it seemed best to give up Buttermere, as the secret valley was beginning to be called, and try to draw the Normans again into the wildest of the passes, where their armour and heavy horses would be a handicap instead of an advantage. No place, however, seemed so defensible as Buttermere, and as it was their depot and arsenal, the Earl decided upon a supreme effort to defend it.

He was himself a shrewd old man whose whole life seemed to have been spent in fighting the Normans. He had a marvellous knowledge of every geographical detail of the Lake country, and seemed to be always ready to suggest some stratagem for the discomfiture of his blood-thirsty enemy. He was a kindly, humorous man, with lightish hair and a

looking north

Papcastle
COCKERMOUTH
River Derwent
River Cocker
Lorton
Grasmoor
Whiteless Pike
site of X battle
Rannerdale Beck
Rannerdale Knotts
Crummock Water
Wood House
Buttermere
Buttermere
HONISTER PASS
Gatesgarth

fresh complexion, long-headed in more senses than one, blue-eyed, tall and active.

He lived in a great manor house built of wood, with a square hole in the roof for smoke, and a fire in the centre of the floor. Instead of windows there were doors of which the top half opened independently of the bottom, and in each corner of the floor there were low walls three or four feet high, enclosing sleeping places filled with rugs and skins —snug beds, well protected from the draughts.

The manor house grew, because when extensions were needed they were built upon the lean-to principle, with doors into the main house. None could say that it was inconvenient either for Summer or Winter, or for the great gatherings where there were eating and drinking, or for the conferences where speeches were made. Nothing is left of it now except the name of the Wood House, but there is a manor of the same period still to be seen in Norway, as well as lesser houses which show how people lived so long ago.

The Church or Chapel in those days was up at Gatesgarth, and the valley was full of little wooden houses, for timber was plentiful in this most beautiful of all the valleys. The bakery and armoury stood where three tracks met, near the water-mill up the lovely glen where a good hotel now stands. There were sheep and swine on the hills, fields of oats and rye, and a deal of work and trade, so that a whole generation existed there in health and strength, helping the war in all their various ways.

Everybody knew that sooner or later the valley would be attacked from the North, but the novel defence which the Earl had been perfecting for years gave them confidence, and even when the great day came and the mothers and children were ordered to the hills they went reluctantly.

This defence which pleased them so much was nothing less than the diversion of the road or track from over the shoulder of Rannerdale Knotts, near the lake, to a narrow and dangerous valley close at hand, where everything was prepared for a great killing.

On a cloudless Summer day the great Norman army set forth from Cockermouth, under the command of Ranulf Meschin, Earl of Carlisle, and marched south to attack the secret valley. The first clash with the English came at Brackenthwaite, where the Normans won an expensive victory. Next day Ranulf pushed on with a diminished army.

Rannerdale Knotts are like a series of knuckles crowning a long ridge with precipitous sides. The hill provides a splendid view, though not much more than a thousand feet high; and it seems to hang over Crummock Water while the country is spread like a map from the Solway to Great Gable, which is the centre of everything in Lakeland.

Here sat Earl Boethar with his son Gille, and his trusty brother Ackin watching the approach of the Norman army. The night had been spent in re-organisation instead of sleep, and now all was ready for the supreme struggle.

The mounted archers were falling back before the Normans as before, and they were keeping away from the lake, as they well knew that their task was to draw the enemy up Rannerdale to the prepared positions. Many a good shot they got in with their clumsy-looking bows, which the Normans had once derided, but long afterwards adopted; and they were well content when the advance guard drove them to the lower slopes of Whiteless Pike, with Rannerdale at their feet, and the false road showing the enemy the way to nowhere.

The pick of the English army, however, lay out of sight near Crummock Water, and they could have held the point against the whole Norman host if it had tried to get round or over it by the old route. Such a thing was, however, only likely to happen if some traitor had betrayed the preparations, and none of the poor souls that the Normans captured would be likely to say a word even under torture.

As the army approached a strong Norman scouting party came along the lakeside, and examined this point where the precipitous rock ran out into the lake. They found that there was no shallow water, and no danger from that quarter, except for as many enemies as might come round in boats. Leaving a score of men as a guard, they worked along the rock itself towards their left, and apparently decided that it was unclimbable. True they were hampered all the time by the archers who were apparently the only guard, but as there was nothing but bare rock to see, it is not surprising that they had no suspicion. In any case no army could have been taken up the face of the hill.

Slowly the critical moment arrived and passed; the Normans spread more and more to their own left, and kept along the Rannerdale Beck with their centre on the new path. Here and there they could see it a mile ahead, leading straight as they thought to that stronghold which for thirty years had given them so much trouble and loss—a thousand curses upon it.

Perhaps it lay just at the top of that narrow route, perhaps a few miles further on, but in any case it would soon be captured. Ranulf Meschin had seen victories before as well as defeats, and he now felt that the opposition had gone to pieces. There were elaborate earthworks at the entrance to Rannerdale Valley, but they were not resolutely held, and the soldiers of the enemy seemed more concerned to save their skins than had been the case on the previous day.

Doubtless he looked upon this as one of the effects of the

defeat, and of his rapid advance with such a great army. 'So much the worse for them,' he thought, 'if they throw away the chance of defending this narrow valley'; for he had long ago decided to act with the greatest ruthlessness. Man, woman and child, he thought, should be killed, in order to make an end for ever of the difficulty which had nearly ruined his life. Everything in the valley should be burnt, and left ruined for all time, as a monument and a warning of the folly of those who rebelled against the King's Majesty.

He would occupy every corner of his great earldom with a vengeance, and make it pay for all the trouble it had given him; 'vae victis'—what could they expect? At any rate he rode forward as an executioner; he would make an end of them for ever—oh, happy day!

By this time the noble Ranulf and the main part of his army were well within the valley of Rannerdale, and it was evident that the enemy were going to make a stand a little higher up. There were walls and ditches beyond the trees, and they were being held with determination by battle-axe and spear men, covered by archers on the higher ground. The Earl of Carlisle pressed forward as indeed did all ranks, and a massed attack was ordered, so as to get through the valley as quickly as possible.

Suddenly an outcry was heard in the rear. Earl Ackin, with thousands of well-armed men, the pick of his brother's army, had descended the rocks down dangerous paths, or had been put round the point in boats and rafts, so that a swarm of them had charged through the camp followers, and, being joined by men waiting on the opposite side of the valley, had occupied an earthwork which had been made for the purpose, and they were already pressing forward so as to cramp and crush the Normans into one another's way, and these, being taken by surprise, were not unanimous about what was to be done first.

Simultaneously the English on all sides threw themselves into the attack and disclosed their great numbers, swollen in the rear ranks by women. Thus Ranulf found himself in a narrow place, surrounded by an unexpected multitude of enemies. It was like a bad dream; all was chaos and terror, for none knew whether to push forward or rush backward towards more open ground. Thus they became massed together and got into each other's way as Boethar and Ackin had expected.

Loud signals were given with horns, and at different points well-armed and armoured men fell into a Norse formation like a spear-head, and pushed forward among the Normans, left-handed men to the left, right-handed to the right, champion axe-wielders at the apex, pushing forward into the crowd, knee-deep in dead and dying.

Ranulf decided to get out of this accursed valley, as it was no use trying to push on. His trumpeters sounded the retirement, and thus his formations were reversed and everything was blocked.

The spear-heads cut into them in all directions, the archers on the ridge were reinforced by women and poured arrows into the mass, while from the slopes of Whiteless Pike and Grassmoor there was a wild pressure of fearless men exulting in the great killing.

Earl Boethar was on Rannerdale Ridge directing the battle beneath him, and very soon he launched his final weapon against the Normans. This consisted of a crowd of wild berserkers, who rushed down the slopes to where the confusion was greatest, and made particularly for the horses of the great Norman knights. These berserkers were half drunken with some spirit which made them impervious to pain; they were fleet of foot and lightly armed, and whenever they could they slipped in and made for the big horses, which they disembowelled as they passed beneath their bellies.

Their reckless bravery helped the terror which spread amongst the Frenchmen as they tried to get out of the valley, and finally a panic seized them. 'Sauve qui peut,' was the cry, and their power of resistance was at an end.

Thousands flung themselves upon Earl Ackin's barrier of men, who in an orgy of killing were pressed back foot by foot. Their weapons were blunted, their strength was worn away, and at last the line began to break.

Some berserker got under the horses of Ranulf himself and his companions, and slashed them as he passed. Down they went, and the great noble tasted the terrors of meaner men. Some faithful servitor helped him up, and a subordinate gave up his horse to him. Ranulf had no idea now but to save himself; he got out of the press, avoided the men on foot, and galloped to Lorton, then made his way to Cockermouth and to disgrace.

Thus ended the last attempt that was made to conquer Earl Boethar, and Lakeland remained at peace until King Stephen, long afterwards, ceded it to Scotland, with Carlisle and the Eden valley, and the country up to Alston, where there were silver mines.

Ranulf Meschin lived under a cloud until 1120, when he was allowed to succeed a relative as Earl of Chester; for he had friends and connections at Court, and there were many who did not blame him overmuch for having failed to subjugate the men of the mountains.

7
Christmas Feast
HUGH WALPOLE

There is always a powerful temptation to find or make heroes in a county like this. Men whose stamina matches the mountains and whose ingenuity emulates the trickeries of valleys. Thorstein of the Mere *was a hero almost included but in the end he had to be left out. A pity because his author, W. G. Collingwood, had two other claims to fame—as a founder of the local archaeological and antiquarian society especially concerned with the uncovering of the Roman Wall; and as the father of R. G. Collingwood the historian. But* Thorstein *had to go, as had* Hope the Hermit *by Edna Lyall, and even* Red Ike. *By no means a great novel, not even a very good novel,* Red Ike *none the less has a bounce about it which helps to explain its enormous popularity in this district— perhaps because the idea of poaching is so attractive to country people (the father of one of the authors—J. M. Denwood—was imprisoned several times for poaching). But* Red Ike *is not just a poacher—he's an attempt to imagine a free spirit still constrained by decent innocence and old nobility. He's a dream, in a way, of what many young men brought up inside these hills, might long to be. The book was first published nearly fifty years ago, with a foreword by Hugh Walpole.*

When Walpole published his own Rogue Herries, *there were distinguished English critics willing to compare it with the greatest novels ever written. It would be difficult to find anyone to do that now; and quite hard, within the present literary establishment, to find anyone prepared to consider his prodigious output 'seriously' at all. Fashions change; and change again. I would make no large claims for him either, except to record the enthusiasm with which I read him as a boy, and propose that no collection such as this could be without Francis Herries—the tormented gentleman who came to hew out a place for himself in Borrowdale.*

STATESMAN PEEL'S HOUSE, BORROWDALE

The Christmas Feast was at its height. This was a scene from Breughel. The trestle tables were piled with food, pies and puddings, hams and sides of beef. The drink was for the most part ale, but there was creeping into the valley now that new destroying devil of the English countryside, the demon gin. There were signs of it here tonight—men were pressing the girls now, their faces flushed, their hands fumbling for breast and side. The women were giggling, the dogs snapping at food and legs and one another. An old man with long white hair, thin as a scarecrow, was dancing very solemnly alone in the middle of the floor, twisting his body into corkscrew shapes. At a table near the chimney a group of old people were playing at cards. But wildness was coming in, coming in from the caverns of the hill, and the high, cold spaces round Sprinkling Tarn and the lonely passes above the listening valleys. It was Christ's Day no longer. He had been turned out when the wind had changed, and all the doors and shutters of the house had rattled their shoulders at His going.

Peel himself felt perhaps that his hand was losing its hold on the scene. And perhaps he did not care. He was a man of his time, and that was a rough time, a cruel and a coarse. They had a small, wild, starving dog, strayed in from the valley, and they had tied him to the leg of a table, and were holding meat just beyond his nose, while he yelped in his agony of hunger, and his little fierce protesting eyes darted wildly about the room.

Up in the half-darkness of the hallan one of the shepherds was stripping to a whispering group of men and girls to show his tattooed body, made when he was in the Indies, as a boy, marvellous, they say, a whole love-story on his legs and back. Although the night was bitter, couples twined closely together wandered out of the house up the road, kissing to the eternal murmur of the running water.

Then the house-door burst wide and a strange crew broke

into the room. They came shouting, singing and very drunk. Their shoulders were powdered with snow, and their frosty breath blew in clouds about them. This was a party that had ridden over from Keswick and Portinscale and Grange, had found their way under the moon to Rosthwaite, and now, drinking at every stage, were turning back again (an they were sober enough to ride) to Keswick. Here was the Lord of Misrule and his followers, a young fellow with very flushed face, a crown awry on his crooked wig, his clothes of purple satin and gold, carried on the shoulders of four half-naked men blacked like Indians and followed by a motley baggage-heap dressed fantastically as jesters, China-men and clowns. There was a Hobby-horse and old Father Neptune with his trident. They burst the doors, then paused to arrange their procession. The naked Indians threw off their cloaks in which they had been wrapped against the cold, caught up their young Lord of Misrule and shouldered him, and so marched up the room, followed by the Jester with his bauble, a lady with a flaxen wig and very naked bosom, Neptune and a posturing, shouting throng.

The natives of the valley drew back against the wall. Here were foreigners from the town, and though their intrusion was no new thing at a Christmas time, yet it boded no good. It had ended before in a bloody riot and so might do again. Francis had been looking for his children, and finding them had bidden David take his sisters home, then, if he would, return. So he was once again alone, a great stillness in his heart in the midst of the riot....

Watching this new invasion he found that he recognized three at least of the company, two from Keswick. The Lord of Misrule himself was young Cuthbertson, son of a wealthy merchant; one of the black men young Fawcett, a Squire's eldest boy; and the Jester himself with his cap and bells Osbaldistone from Threapthwaite, near Whitehaven. Young Osbaldistone was often at Keswick, and Herries had been with him at cards and cock-fighting. There was no love between them. Herries had won his money, which the young fool could ill afford to lose, and Herries had kissed a girl that Osbaldistone had also been pursuing.

At the sight of him a spasm of revolt and disgust caught his heart. He had drunk nothing: he had been moved tonight

by the courteous friendliness of Peel, by the happy simplicity
of the earlier part of the evening, and, at this last, by his
meeting with the child. Apart and reserved as he seemed
standing there alone, yet his heart had been filled with kindli-
ness and an almost child-like desire to be friends with the
world.

At the sight of this rabble he was tempted to slip away and
find his bed. Had he gone, the whole course of his life would
have been other. Nevertheless our lives are dictated by
character, not by chance. Some foolish pride kept him. He
fancied that from the corner by the fire-window the pedlar
sardonically watched him. It was true that many eyes were
on him, as they had been all the evening; so, because he had
some conceit and felt a challenge in the air, he stayed.

Events followed then with dreamlike swiftness. Afterwards if he ever looked back to this night it seemed to him
that he had from the very first been trapped. He could not
have escaped; he did not pity himself for this (in all his life-
history from the first page to the last there was no self-pity),
but he did ask himself whether he could have avoided the
event; he could not.

The procession settled itself about its Lord: drink was
brought: there was much sham ceremony: subjects knelt and
sentences were passed; the lady in cloth of gold with the
naked bosom was proclaimed Queen. The peasants stood
around, mouths agape, the little wild dog, who had been
forgotten, yelped dismally, then broke his rope, crawled to
a corner where he feasted ravenously. Everyone was at ease
again. Dancing took the floor. Figures, fantastic, painted in
orange and scarlet and purple, laughing, singing, kissing,
whirled and turned; some fell upon the floor and lay there.
Still in the farther corner the old people, like characters
painted on the wall, played gravely at their cards.

Young Osbaldistone, his cap awry, the laced waistcoat
unbuttoned, pursued a girl and encountered Herries. He
stopped short.

Herries gravely bowed. Osbaldistone looked. The drink
cleared from his eyes. He straightened himself. He was a
cold-tempered, severe lad in his natural life, debauched
enough but ready at any moment to clear debauchery from
his system. He stood back fumbling the hilt of his sword.

'Mr Francis Herries.'

'Mr Richard Osbaldistone.'

He yet stuttered a little. The drink was not all cleared. 'Dick to my friends,' then added softly, 'but not to you, Mr Herries.'

No one heard him. Herries frowned. He did not want a quarrel with the boy here, not tonight, Christmas night, and in Peel's house. He bowed.

'I wish you good evening,' he said and turned.

Osbaldistone touched his shoulder. Herries, turning back, was amazed at the hatred that formed and edged the other's face like a mask. To hate him like that! And for what? For nothing—a loss at cards, a girl's kiss. No—for what he himself in his very spirit was. And at the consciousness of that his heart sank and his anger grew.

'You will not wish me good evening,' Osbaldistone said. 'I will have no good evening from you. Since our meeting of last week I have been determined on a word with you. You are a cheat, Mr Herries, a liar and—it may be—a coward. For the last we will see.'

Then he raised his hand and struck Herries's cheek. Miraculously, this, too, no one saw. It gave the dreaminess of this strange hour an added colour—the shrill, discordant music of the violin, the thick steaming air, the great chimney with its smoky fire, the figures confused in colour, unreal in chin and eye and limb, the movement striving, it seemed, to make significant pattern—and yet Herries quite alone in a frozen place with this boy who hated him.

But no man had ever struck him and had no answer. He frowned sternly on young Osbaldistone, who was breathing now fiercely as though driven by some terrific emotion.

'Not here,' he said quietly. 'There is a green behind the house. The moon is bright. I will join you there in an instant. But take care; we must go separately. My host tonight is my friend.'

At once, again as in a dream, young Osbaldistone had disappeared. Herries looked about him. Oh! how desperately he did not wish this to happen! It was from no fear for himself. But he seemed to be haunted tonight by the past; something was pulling him back into that other life that he had abandoned; something would not let him escape.

But he must find a second. It must be, if possible, someone not from Keswick. The less that this was known ... He turned towards the door and saw the pedlar standing against the wall, smiling ironically and stroking his thighs with his hands.

'You can do me a service,' Herries said. The pedlar followed him out. The moon was full. No snow was falling.

Against the green behind the house everything was marked as though it had been cut from black paper, the ridge of hill, the roof-line, the thick wall of jagged stones.

Osbaldistone was waiting there and Fawcett, a stout, plump youth, absurd with his blackened face and thick cloak heavily furred. He came to Herries.

'For God's sake, Mr Herries, this must be avoided ...' His teeth were chattering.

'Too damned cold for talk,' said Osbaldistone.

They spoke in whispers.

'If Mr Osbaldistone will apologize for his insult,' said Herries.

'I will not,' said Osbaldistone.

They faced one another: every detail in the scene was clear under the moon. It was indeed bitterly cold. The frost seemed to creep upon the flat stones that lay about the field. Herries was aware of the tiniest details and would remember them all his days. A snail-track glittered in crystal on the farm wall behind him; a little wind ran over the grass, fluttering the light snow that lay loosely on the ground, and on the path beyond the field he could see the moonlight shine on the ice that the cold was forming on the little pools.

They advanced. At once he knew that Osbaldistone was no swordsman—and a moment later Osbaldistone knew it too. Again the thought tapped Herries's heart: 'How he must hate me to run this crazy risk!' and again 'Why?' In another moment or two he was aware of the sword's instinct, something much more deadly and determined than his own. He could never strike another's weapon with his and not feel that separate aliveness in his blade, as though it said: 'You have called me out. You have liberated me. Now I am my own master.' And now he was very curiously aware that he must restrain this creature, use all his force and power, otherwise the boy would be hurt. But as they parried and struck and parried again a warmth of companionship with his sword swelled in his throat as though it had said to him: 'Come. We are comrades now. We march together. You wouldn't desert me when you have brought me so far.'

His pride in his accomplishment grew in him. His body grew warm, taut, eager. He forgot his opponent, felt only the moon shining above that cold field, the splendid panoply of stars exulting in his skill.

He had the boy utterly at his mercy, and, at the same moment, the boy's face swung down to him as though it had been lowered from a height. He gazed into it and saw terror there, the certain expectation of instant death.

Death. Yes, one more link in the ridiculous binding chain. This time at least he would be master of his fortune.

He lowered his blade and stepped back. An instant later Osbaldistone's sword had carved his right cheek in two, a deep riven cut from temple to chin.

His face was flooded with blood. Dropping his sword, the field whirling about his ears like a top, he sank to his knee.

He heard young Fawcett cry 'Enough...' and a word about honour, then the frosted stones leapt up and hit him into darkness. But before he sank he felt the pedlar's hand on his arm.

8

Like a Little Doll

ELIZABETH A. M. ROBERTS
& 'Mrs N.o.4.'

The voice from the majority—call it the working-classes if you like—has been little heard in literature until the last hundred years or so. What has happened more recently has been the direct recording of 'lives' by interview. I did it myself in Speak for England. *Elizabeth Roberts did it in the Barrow-in-Furness area. Here is one of her interviews where the woman is talking about the attitudes in her childhood home towards sex and death. The time would be about the eighteen-nineties.*

She never told us a word, we knew nothing then.... We used to know how fat mam was getting but we didn't know anything. Then I heard a noise one night and I got up and I thought m' mamma must be bad and I went in the room and said, 'Is m' mamma bad?' Dad said, 'No go and get yourself back into bed m' lass she'll be all right till morning.' When I got up in the morning and went in she had this little baby and it was stillborn. She said, 'You're not going to school today Rose.' I said, 'Aren't I?' She said, 'No you'll have to stay at home I want you to do something for me.' I said, 'What's been the matter with you mamma?' She said, 'Well I've got a baby.' I said, 'Where is it?' She said, 'It's just there,' and it was on a wash stand, on a pillow with a cover over it. When I looked at it it was like a little doll, very small. She said, 'I want you to go to a shop and ask for a soap box.' I said, 'A soap box mam.' She said, 'Yes.' I said, 'What's it for?' She said, 'To put that baby in.' I brought this soap box

back and I called on the road to my friend, a young girl I
went with, so I told her and she went with me. She said, 'I'll
come down to your house with you.' She came and we had
a look at this little doll and my friend said, 'Let us line this
little box with wadding.' We lined this box with this bit of
wadding and then m' mamma put this wee baby in it and the
lid fastened down like the boxes do today, no nails. She
said, 'There's a letter here . . .' They didn't call them mid-
wives then, just ladies and it used to be half a crown or five
shillings to come and deliver a baby. She gave me a letter,
'Now you've got to go up the cemetery and give this letter
to the grave digger, any grave digger you see in.' I said, 'I
can't take it wrapped up in paper' so I went in the back and
saw an old coat of m' dad's. I ripped the black lining out
of this coat and we wrapped this little box in this lining and
put some string round it, put it under our arms and off we
went to the grave digger. I give him this letter and he read
it. He said, 'Oh yes, just take it over in the church porch
love. You'll see a few parcels in that corner, just leave it there.'
Me being inquisitive said, 'What are you going to do with it?'
He said, 'Well we have public graves, everybody don't buy
graves they haven't the money, when the public graves get
nearly full up we put one in each grave.' 'Oh that's what
you do,' I said. He said, 'Yes. Tell your mammy it'll be all
right,' and we turned back home.

Did it upset you at the time?

Yes, because we thought it was like a little doll. It wasn't
really developed, just small.

How old would you be then?

I'd be about twelve.

9

Black Pheasants

BETTY WILSON

You cannot escape the dialect if you get anywhere near the heart of Cumberland. It has existed as a suppressed and outlawed language for over nine hundred years and despite all the efforts of governments, schools and socially conscious mothers it still has a daily life, especially on the tongues of children. Betty Wilson's Cumberland tales are justly the best-loved of the dialect stories. They were written last century by Thomas Farrell of Aspatria. Black Pheasants has the additional advantage of showing the rustic putting one over on the metropolitan—a triumph still nurtured by many countrymen.

Ov aw t' fwoaks o' Emmelton, Widdup, or Secmurder, theear nivver was a fellah keener o' devarshun nor ooar Bob. A gud temper't swort ov a chap he was, to be shure; helpy amang t' nabours; 'onest as t' day's leet; an' a gud wurker when he hed a mind; but somehow or udder, t' mind was seldom theer when t' hay was i' dry cock, or t' cworn ruddy for hoosin'. He wad git up seún i' t' mwornin', an' toak as if he wad duah aw ov a day, an' wad git his brekfast, an' ga reet off till Widdup Mill, or t' Blùe Bell, or t' Peel Wyke, an' mebbe drink a full week. Sumtimes he tel't us aw his rises ower ov a neet, an' sum ov them war queer enéuf, Ah duah ashure yê.

    Well, menny a 'ear sen, Bob was drinkin' at t' Peel Wyke two or three days just aboot mid-summer, when he could ill be spar't at heám, but what càr't Bob for that. At that time

t' cwoach-horses used to be chàng't at Smiddy Green, an'
Jobby Hodgin waitit on them—seah yê may kalkilate it
wasn't yisterday.

Pooar Willy Harvey keep't t' Peel Wyke, an' him an' Bob
was toakin' just as oald Deavy Jonson druv' up. Oot gits a
fellah wid a dubble-barrel't gun, an' two greet ghem bags
strap't ower his shooders. He was varra polite, an' noddit,
an' ran back an' forret, prancin' like a cat on a het gúrdel.

Well, ooar Bob cudn't mak oot what he was efter, seah bê
way of introdukshun, Bob ses,

'Gâun ta shût, mister?'

'Yes,' sed he.

'What ur yê gâun ta shût at this time o' t' 'ear?'

'O, fessents,' ses he.

'Fessents! at this season?' sed Bob. 'Wey man, they're just
breedin', an' if yê war to kill yan noo, ye wad be teán ta
Cockermuth in a crack.'

At this, t' fellah leùkt rayder doon i' t' mooth, leetit a segar,
tùk a drink ov his yal, an', efter puffin' away for ten minnets,
ses he, 'It's a bad job.'

Bob ses, 'What is?'

'Well,' he ses, in his oan mak o' toak, mind 'Ah was
stoppin' at t' Bush Hotel, at Carel, last neet, an' a lot o'
fellahs an' me got on toakin' aboot fessents, an' Ah sed theear
was hundreds aboot Widdup, an' they aks't hoo Ah knew;
an' Ah sed Ah'd seen them. They rayder disputit me wurd.
Seah at last, fra' less ta mair, Ah bet them fifty pund at Ah
wad shùt two duzzen afooar tomorrah neet. Noo, they wad
likely know weel eneuf 'at it wasn't t' season; neahboddy
wad let me shút an' as ther war nin ta be gitten wid silver
gun, that is, wid munney, they wad win their wager.'

Well, t' fellah humm't an' he haw't, an' toak't mighty
fine, for Bob cudn't tell hoaf o' what he sed, an' t' reason a'
this was, 'at he com' fra' Lunnun. He caw't his-sel sum-at
like a Cocker.

'Neah matter,' thow't Bob, 'whether thoo's cocker, setter,
or spaniel; bit Ah know ya thing thoo is, an' that's a big
feúl.' Yit Bob didn't say seah; let Bob alèan for that; his
pokkets wer' empty, an' his pint full, at t' Cocker's expense.
It wadn't answer ta 'frunt him, at least nut than. Seah they
sat an' supp't an' crack't on till towards eight o'clock, t' fellah

vārra nār bet what ta duah, an' Bob hardly knowin' hoo ta help him, nor, Ah dar say, nut carin' a heap as lang as his pint was full.

At last t' Cocker says, 'If you'll help ta git meh a quantity o' fessents, Ah'll give yê five pund for yer labor.'

Well, five pund sartinly was a tempter for Bob, 'at hed sitten two or three days, owder on sumboddy's cwoat lap, or hed been hingin' up, as t' sayin' is, aback o' t' bar dooar. Than Bob begins to ask t' fellah if ivver he'd poach't enny, an' he sed he hedn't, nor he'd nivver shûtten enny fessents bit yance, when he fand sum yung uns in t' nest in a tree, an' shot them throo t' branches.

'Fessents' nests in a tree?' ses Bob.

'Yes,' ses t' Cocker.

Bit t' truth just than flashed across Bob's mind 'at t' fellah didn't know a fessent when he saw yan, seah Bob consider't a bit, an' at last he ses,

'Well, Ah mun try ta help yê; we'll sit till barrin' up time, an' than we'll off when aw's whyet.'

Than, efter revivin' t' deed yal 'at was i' ther stommaks wid a sup o' Mrs Harvey's rum, away they went sneakin' off at t' deed time o' neet, bent on plunder. Theer was neah boddy ta bodder them much i' them days, an' they nobbet met oald Ann Simpson till they gat till t' pleáce whoar t' fessents war.

T' Cocker ses, 'They shurely sit nar t' hooses.'

'Oh, ay,' ses Bob, 'clwose till.'

Well, Bob gat furst up yá tree, an' than anudder, an' fand burds plenty. He twin't ther necks roond, an' threw them doon, an' t' Cocker pop't them intill t' bags.

'Clean full,' ses t' Cocker at last.

'Aw reet,' ses Bob.

Wi' that he com doon t' tree, an' away they sally't off ta t' Peel Wyke. T' Cocker went ta bed, an' Bob laid on t' swab aw neet; seún i' t' mwornin' t' Cocker gat up an' order't breakfast for two. Ham an' eggs an' a chop, an' Ah know nut what, was neah deef nut for Bob ta crack, seah efter he'd whyte astonish't t' Cocker be cleanin' up ivvery plate, they coontit t' burds ower, an' fand they hed two duzzen, an' ten ta beùt.

'Stop,' ses Bob, 'we mun put a lock o' shot in them.'

Well, they hung them up be t' waw side, an' smatter't away at them till they war gaily well riddel't.

Than t' Cocker drew oot five golden sover'ns an' gev them ta Bob, paid for him a gùd dinner an' a bottle o' rum; an' just wi' that t' cwoach druv up. In gat t' Cocker wid his burds, an' as t' horses mov't off, he wav't his hat, an' mead his-sel varra daft.

Whedder he wan his bet wid his BLACK FESSENTS nowder Bob nor me ivver hârd tell; bit Ah think Carel fwoak wad know 'at they war nobbet *Crows!*

Spring
in Borrowdale
GRAHAM SUTTON

O. S. Macdonell, Halliwell, Sutcliffe, Constance Howe, H. de Vere Stacpoole—these and many others set novels up here but most of them throw a light only in a local context. Few leap across the boundary. Graham Sutton might be thought an exception. He wrote several novels which chronicle the fortunes of the Fleming family. In this extract from North Star there is the bonus that the 'Hartley' character is the son of Coleridge; and so, in the work of a twentieth-century novelist, the Lake poets take yet another bow.

Spring came to Borrowdale with a beauty to twist the heart: and nowhere welcomer than at Seathwaite, where from All Saints to Lady Day the impending mountains robbed them of sunlit hours. For now a mist of tender bronze began to suffuse their birches; now there were primroses, in Johnny Wood and the dell below Seat Oller; the ouzel piped from hidden gills, and the cuckoo was shouting all day long from the blind end of their valley. Soon when they came out after breakfast to work they saw—past their stone walls, past brown fields lately ploughed by Dirck—the hanging coppices over Rosthwaite, sombre and purple-grey: till sunlight touched them, and against last year's oak-scrub the young birches showed brilliantly, puff-balls of emerald fire.

At Seathwaite they counted Lady Day the turn of the year. And to Ewan particularly it arrived as harbinger of two pleasures: Clute's birthday, which by a delectable coincidence fell on the first of April; and his own, drawing calculably

nearer, which came in mid-May towards the end of the lamb-
ing. Moreover, this year brought the extra fun of young
Hartley's return to Keswick. Since Michaelmas, Hartley had
been at school; but he was back now on holiday at his Uncle
Southey's, and the boys planned long days.

'Why is it Sprinkling?' Hartley inquired. They lay and
sunned themselves at the narrow end of the tarn: their secret
end, which a rock-rib hid cunningly from the track to
Eskhause.

Ewan said: 'My father told me that it used to be Sparkling
—his father always called it that. I suppose it got changed to
match the fell.'

'Sprinkling Fell—Sprinkling—Sparkling Tarn? No,
Sprinkling's right!' declared Hartley. 'What rum things
words are! You can shuffle them round and try them in
different patterns, but there's always just one.' And Ewan
thought enviously: Young Hartley should know, if anyone
does! He's got plenty to choose from.... For Hartley, at
Ewan's age, had acquired a remarkable vocabulary from the
poets and learned men who assembled at Uncle Southey's:
and could argue with them on their pet subjects: and wrote
poetry of his own. His talk with Ewan gave him an inspiration now, for he said suddenly: 'I'd like to make a poem that
should be a symphony of fell-names.'

'It 'ud have to be a long poem!'

'Oh, I'd not want to use them all. There's one called
Robinson, up Newlands: Robinson! What a crime——'

'What's your school like?' asked Ewan. In secret he was a
little jealous of the school that kept Hartley from him. Young
Hartley, for all his big dark eyes and his round baby-face
and childish looks, was excitingly mature: far more mature
than anybody in Borrowdale, except Uncle Charles: yet not
in the least like Uncle Charles, for he chattered continually
of literature and musicians, and of men who worked for the
newspapers, and of philosophy—a subject apparently which
his father professed and wrote. 'Is it fun at school?' Ewan
repeated.

'Not very. It's extremely puerile, and you're never left
to yourself. Though it's a change from High Art and
High Thinking at Uncle Southey's; school life is frankly
low.'

Ewan said: 'You're lucky, meeting people who do curious things for a living.'

'What do you want to do?'

'That's just it—how can I find out! Up here they don't know anything about anything except farming. They've heard of journalists and painters and poets, but they can't say how anybody starts to be one—and they think it's all rather dangerous.'

'I think *you*'re lucky,' Hartley told him. 'Your people are all so calm and right. You do things, instead of arguing how they ought conceivably to be done. Everyone says your father's one of the best sheepmasters in the country; and your mother—d'you know she is called the Beauty of Borrowdale? As for your marvellous Uncle Clute——! He's *your* schoolmaster, isn't he? I mean you've had him for a tutor, instead of being sent to school?'

'I suppose so. He's taught me to read and write, and arithmetic and some history. But it's not like school really, we just do it for fun.'

'Well, there you are! My teachers don't know what fun is; they're either childish as I said—as if they had never grown up—or they're antediluvian.'

'They're what?'

'Old women, bound in calf—rather shabbily. But I luxuriate in Uncle Clute, he's so—urbane's the word, do you think? He's miraculous. He lives up here and he never seems to go anywhere, but you can see he's infinitely more a man of the world than these—these perambulating garrulous wiseacres.'

Ewan stared.

'That's a phrase of my father's,' Hartley explained. 'I fancy *he* finds Uncle Southey's circus rather a bore at times, and that's why he melts away so often, lecturing or—just visiting. And you know that's another thing I envy you——' He looked suddenly wistful. 'You have your father all the time; and he's such good friends with your mother.'

'She's not my mother,' Ewan put in. 'That's why I call her Jennifer.' Hartley seemed mystified.

'Yes? But you call your father Dirck——'

'She's no relation,' Ewan said. 'If she was, Uncle Charles would be my grandfather, but he isn't.'

Hartley broke into his bubbling laugh. 'He's either your grandfather or nothing; so you call him your uncle, just to make it more difficult! How ingeniously baffling—I say, am I being too inquisitive?'

'No. But it isn't baffling either; Dirck married my mother first.'

'Is she—dead, then?' asked Hartley, subdued.

Ewan nodded. 'Oh, yes. So we sold up, and moved here where Uncle Charles and Jennifer lived, and Dirck married Jennifer—and that's all.'

'What made your mother die, d'you think?'

'I don't know,' said Ewan curtly. 'They never told me.'

'I expect,' Hartley sympathised, 'that she fell into a decline. Ladies do that.'

'They never talk about those days,' went on Ewan. 'And I can't talk to them about my future because they don't *know* —they don't know anything outside sheep. That's where you're luckier! If you decide to be a poet——'

'What about Uncle Clute?'

'Well, yes——' admitted Ewan rather reluctantly. 'He has talked to me about painting; he's a painter himself, you know.'

'Indeed I didn't!' Hartley exclaimed with interest. 'What does he paint?'

'Oh, landskips for caterpillars—for the summer visitors, I should say. But he won't sign them; and he keeps rubbing into me, he's no artist; he says he only paints for cash—what are you laughing at?'

'At the only! Why else should any one paint? If you heard the humdudgeon that they talk at Greta Hall about art—and they all end by asking Uncle Southey to advance them five guineas! By jove, I'd take your Uncle Clute's advice on art before theirs——'

'You wouldn't on poetry,' put in Ewan. 'He's says himself he doesn't know a thing about poetry, except Shake-speare——'

'Well, that's a beginning.'

'But I mean modern poetry. You see I'd rather write than paint, if I thought I could live on that—and your father lives on it, doesn't he?'

'Not altogether,' explained Hartley. 'He lives on literary

composition in general—and of course, on his friends. Luckily we have lots of friends. But his poetry is well thought of. Have you read *Lyrical Ballads* yet?'

'I'm afraid not. Were those his poems?'

'A few. The rest were Mr Wordsworth's. *I* think my father's *Ancient Mariner* is worth the lot of 'em rolled together —but don't tell Mr Wordsworth that; he is apt to turn a little bleak if he hears our *Mariner* too much praised. And he's written a most magnificent one, a Chinese one called *Kubla Khan*, not published yet, that he dreamt in a sort of vision——'

'Mr Wordsworth or——'

'Goodness, no! *He'd* never have written *Kubla Khan*, he hasn't the imagination.'

'Does your father have—visions?' Ewan asked curiously.

'Not prophetic ones, no. But he's endowed with a remarkably prolific imagination—I find that poetry needs imagination,' young Hartley added, gazing at Ewan with his round face cupped in his hands. 'Have you got any?' But without waiting for an answer he hurried on: 'Some people say my father's uniquity in that respect is because he takes laudanum —a pity, I always think. He can't really need it; I have an excellent imagination myself, and I don't take laudanum. . . . Oh, it's a drug, it makes you dream, like he dreamt *Kubla*. Do you know Dungeon Gill?'

Ewan shook his head.

'It's in Langdale, down there—some day we'll go, and I'll read you the part of *Kubla* that pictures it.'

'But you said *Kubla* was Chinese?'

'It is. Only there's a description of an abyss in it (do you say abbis or abiss?) exactly like Dungeon Gill; he was writing a story-poem about Langdale then and they overlapped, I dare say. That's how *my* imaginations work—they grow, and burn in me and I can't tell what they'll be up to next, and sometimes two get entangled. Do yours do that?'

Ewan considered it. 'I think I hear them more like voices, arguing with each other; because they never agree. It's like a duel fought with voices——'

'Yes, of course! Words are swords——'

'But they're not matched like swords,' went on Ewan. 'Two fellows duelling with a knife and an axe: or say, cutlass and horsewhip. They're distinct and—and dangerous in quite different ways: because the voices are different. A bright voice arguing with a thundery angry voice, or a cruel voice with a scared one——'

Hartley's big dark eyes widened. 'I see! They are sounds, with you; my imaginations are pictures——'

'And at the end,' said Ewan, 'one voice swings round—that's after he's turned to go away—and kills the other with a sort of thrust of his words: like a fighter that runs you through.'

'Ye-es: I've heard actors do it that way,' Hartley agreed. 'Do you ever see play-actors?'

'What, in Borrowdale!' They both laughed.

'Never mind!' said Hartley. 'I've a particularly good imagination in stock, I invented it yesterday; let's find some narrow twisty gill, and we'll act it as we go home.'

On their way down, Ewan found him the very spot they wanted. Between steep red banks, edged with grass against the sky and choked at their base with stones, the beck had scooped a long ravine full of bends and fresh vistas. Hartley expounded the imagination to Ewan as they clambered down the steep bed.

'It's behind us—It's pad-padding after us!' he said. He whispered: 'It is called the Rabzeze Kallaton; It has flat pale feet—and Its bones are outside Its skin!' He was hurrying Ewan forward. 'Don't look round, don't look round! That's fatal—and you'd see nothing anyway, It's too sly. Shall I tell you Its ghastly method? Between each corner It runs a little —lumbery but quick—so It keeps close behind us; but before each, It stops and—and sniggers in Its proboscis, because It knows that It can catch us any time that It likes! And there's only one way to deal with It—but the risk's terrible——'

'Here, I say——' Ewan quavered.

'Keep on! Faster, faster, till we reach the first rowan tree.' He clutched Ewan's arm suddenly. 'O Ewan, is there a rowan tree? O God, please, please let there be a rowan tree or we're doomed!'

'Past yon shoulder!' cried Ewan. He knew, of course, that this was only one of young Hartley's games but he was frightened in the dark gill. Now they could see the rowans ahead, pale-stemmed like skeletons.

'Ten seconds!' Hartley panted. 'Five seconds—*now*!' He grabbed Ewan, spun round facing up the gill, and extended his forefingers. 'Kallaton, apagé!' he screamed out.

Both boys stood stockstill. Hartley was pale, and trembled. They could hear their hearts thumping as they watched the bend of the gill. At last: 'Ah, it's worked again!' Hartley whispered. 'We're safe—this time. Only let's get out, quick, quick!'

They clawed their way out of the gill and emerged on the fellside. Here in the open Ewan began to feel ashamed of the fright he had had. 'I say, you *are* an ass!' he told Hartley. But he noticed that Hartley was as white as milk, and for some minutes neither of them spoke again. Then Hartley smiled at him.

'That's never failed, so far,' he said: 'only there must be rowans! If there are, and you stand and *think* at It when It's just going to turn the corner, It has misgivings and goes back.'

'And supposing it didn't?' Ewan grinned. Hartley jumped up.

'Then I presume our only practicable course would be to run like the devil—come on, I'll race you to that rock!'

Ewan beat him by yards. As they went on down into Borrowdale he said casually: 'That game of yours—it's funny, I've always hated being followed by anything, ever since I was little; it makes me feel angry inside.'

'Angry—or frightened?'

'Of course not frightened! At least—oh well, anyhow I don't like it.'

Hartley looked curiously at him. 'Listen to this,' he said:

> 'Like one, that on a lonely road
> Doth walk in fear and dread,
> And having once turn'd round, walks on
> And turns no more his head:
> Because he knows, a frightful fiend
> Doth close behind him tread—

That's pretty good, I always think—oh, a thing of my father's.'

'Say it again!' begged Ewan. Hartley did so, and for a long time after he had finished, Ewan stayed silent. At last: 'It's tremendous, it's—terrifying!' he murmured. 'I'll remember that, all my life——'

When they reached Seathwaite they heard Mr Wordsworth's voice indoors, declaiming. Hartley pulled Ewan below the wall. 'It's the Ancient Mariner!' he lamented. 'Let's creep off and hide somewhere.' They retired up the lonnin.

'I thought you said you'd got shut of him?'

'But I did!' answered Hartley peevishly. 'At some yew trees—below the wadd-mine there; he was whelping an ode to *them*.'

'I expect the wadd-miners chased him off. They are pretty warm against trespassers——'

' 'Sst!' Hartley whispered. 'We are betrayed——' Footsteps approached their lair.

'Wait—no, it's only the Frightful Child!' Ewan laid a finger to his lips as Faith appeared round the corner. 'Has he gone?'

'I saw you slink off! No, he's called for *you*,' she told Hartley. 'He said at first he wouldn't wait, when he heard you were up the fell; but he did. He remembered a poetry. He's been reciting it for hours—he can't know much more, surely?'

'Can't he just!' Hartley groaned.

'We'll play at castaways,' Faith suggested. 'I've been out scouting. I've discovered a breadfruit-orchard growing near the lagoon.' She dropped her apron, and showed half a dozen of Jennifer's fresh-baked scones.

'What an invaluable sister!' Hartley ejaculated as they shared the plunder between them. 'That is, if you *are* Ewan's sister?'

'But of course, stupid!' Faith nodded.

'I always understood you were. But I've been hearing such a complicated explanation today——'

'Hoff-hiffa——' said Ewan with his mouth full.

'What?'

'Half-sister——'

'When we're grown up I'm going to marry him,' Faith put in.

Hartley's round eyes twinkled. 'I see: and then you'll call him Uncle Ewan—oh, it's simple, once one gets used to it!'

Before long they heard the gate-latch click, and watched the sturdy form of Mr Wordsworth disappear down the lonnin. Then, whooping, they invaded Jennifer with demands for something to eat.

Snow in February

NORMAN NICHOLSON

Norman Nicholson is the present laureate of the Lakes. His poems have brought him national acknowledgment and well-earned distinction. His prose books on the district are first rate. This is from Provincial Pleasures.

For nearly a week the fist of the frost has held tight to the land. There have been brilliant Candlemas days when the tiles seemed to skip under the whip of the cold. There have been opaque days, when the sky was heaped and blizzarded with snow, and yet the snow did not fall. Only occasional flakes came haphazardly down like white sifts of charred paper when a chimney is on fire. Everywhere else there was snow. Scotland was kilt-deep in it; it was up to the lorry-axles on Shap, up to the bus-steps in London. At Old Trafford it was wicket-high, and in Sussex it was up to the Downs. On the brown fells above the estuary there were chalkings of snow, streaks and hatchings and high-lights. But here all was bare.

Then yesterday morning the wind dodged into the south-west and thaw slithered across the land, and, suddenly, improbably, out of the thawing wind came the snow. It melted as it fell, but not as fast as it fell. Pavements and gutters were filled with cold tapioca pudding.

'This'll soon get away,' everyone said. 'It's wet as muck already. It'll turn to rain in no time.'

But in the evening, under the dark, the gulleys ceased to

drip, the pudding took a crust, and everyone was saying, 'Shouldn't be surprised if it snowed again.'

Yet they *were* surprised. One is always surprised by snow. The streets themselves looked surprised, holding their breath in an anxious hush—a hush which is perhaps the strangest thing about the snow. As you look at the street, seeing movement and hearing none, you feel as if an unnatural deafness had come upon you. Your eyes and your ears do not co-ordinate; it is very much like the sensation of a fever. The chimneys are bewildered, the roofs, slippery and uncertain. Dormer windows prick up their ears like terriers. The birds flop in the snow, learning to ski.

But the snow itself is completely without surprise. I survey it from my bedroom window and everywhere it is quite at home. It lies on the slates, unmarked except by sparrows; it swells and balloons over the edge of the launders. The roofs have lost their straight-line geometry of slant and perpendicular. The chimneys, hung with white soot, jerk up from a Moscow of onion-domed attics. Starlings, blundering among the chimney-pots, precipitate small avalanches over their tails. Jackdaws, trying to settle on the watershed of a roof, find themselves top-heavy and fly away, clacking like nutcrackers. The sparrows alone, with their urchin adaptability, have found their snow legs, and know already that today the street-bottoms are as safe as the air and that they run no danger from dog or bicycle.

The 'lum hats' of the chimney-pots are padded with white felt on the one side. A three-inch ribbon of snow, sideways up, is balanced on the telephone wires until, now and then, a bird lets on them, and ten or twenty yards fall like droppings into the street. The spire of St Kentigern's, seen above the Banks, carries one elongated isosceles triangle of pure white from base to weathercock.

I push open my casement windows, making two carvings of snow tumble from the attic roof into the little balcony above the shop-window. The snow-plough has not yet been round, but already the street is trampled by the men going to work. No school-children so far, but I can hear the first faint scrapes and slushing of householders beginning to clean their pavements, and the sound is strange and hard to recognise in the almost silent air, seeming as if it came from a long distance, a country sound in the wrong place. Old Sprout, the greengrocer, banging the door behind him as he comes out of his shop, loosens half a cart-load of snow, which skids off his roof and pancakes on the pavement, missing his head by no more than a foot.

'Glory!' he says. 'Greenland's icy mountains.'

Half a dozen of Chris Crackenthwaite's apprentices pass down the street just as the girls begin to arrive at the Market Hall factory. At once there is a parabolic storm of snowballs. Head-scarves, bootees, mackintoshes and woollen gloves are whirled and scrimmaged together. The air glistens with screeching. Snowballs explode like white bombs on doors and lamp-posts. Girls, caught by the arm, have snow rubbed into their hair like salt into a herring. Three of them, catching a youth who is trying to push a bicycle through a snow-drift, tip him into the gutter and stuff his shirt with snow. Faces red as holly berries, mouths in a bubble of swearing, they dip and revel in the snow. The Market Clock strikes eight. Shaking the snow off their hair and coats, the girls skitter up the back stairs into the factory. The sparrows once more take possession of the street.

Now it is twelve o'clock and school is out and all those who do not stay behind for dinner are bounding down Trafalgar Street, the little ones paddling up to the Wellington-tops in the drifts left on either side by the snow plough. Ten minutes to shovel in a plateful of hot stew or fish and chips, and then out again into the back streets and down to the Iron Green. The youngest of all have been there all morning, waddling in snow up to their arm-pits. They are no longer playing with it or enjoying it, but try with a numb next-door-to-crying persistence to scramble over the wall and climb the slag-bank. At every step they fall back, foxed and flummoxed by the snow, tripping over buried buckets, breaking their shins on hidden cobbles.

The elder boys are not deterred, however. They know their way about the slag-bank as a shepherd knows his way about the fells. They know every track and ledge in the slag; know how the rain has carved it into gulleys where now the snow lies deep as a crevasse; know how the surface of the slag is in parts rotten as scree, and in others hard as iron.

They know, too, all the secret places of the bank: the nest of sandbags built during the War for the Home Guard; the ruins of Marsh Edge Farm that lies in an angle of the tip hidden from the town; the steps, cut in the slag-face, that lead down to the Ironworks Pier from which they can watch the boats. This slag-bank is very old—belonging, for the most part, to the last years of the last century, when smelting was so extravagant with ore that some people say there was more iron in the slag than in the pig. There has been no tipping here for many years, and already the bank seems to be slowly settling back into the earth from which it came. Today, it is settled entirely, and seems as ancient a part of the landscape as the sea or the fells. The snow drifts against its flanks, and collects in the creases and ghylls which split its sides, and piles up on ledges and parapets and corries. Every now and then clouds of steam from the cooling reservoirs of the furnaces float over the skyline. It is an Icelandic scene of snow and hot-springs, of glacier, rock, cliffs, sky, and seabirds.

The sun comes out, and each boy is cartooned by his ironic shadow, and the willows become black hands clutching up from the snow. The snow-dazzle, here, has the brilliancy and wideness of the Sahara sun, for this part of the town has nothing cramped about it. When the people from Furnace Road visit the new housing estates they feel hemmed in, for though they live in a tight little terrace with backyard behind, and rug-sized gardens in front, they are used to a spaciousness that is due not to planning but to the lack of plan. These small rows of houses look as if they had been dumped down like baggage on a railway platform while the owner goes for a sandwich. Those on Furnace Road face across allotments and melancholy fields, that lead eventually to the mines. The rest face nowhere. And about all of them is the untidy spaciousness of land which has been forgotten, greens, allotments, sumps, dumps, and slag-holes. *The Furnace Arms* stands solid and square as a block of concrete, its door and eight windows marking right-angles of shadow in the gleaming stucco. It looks as isolated as an eighteenth-century farmhouse among the fells. Indeed, it is very like a farmhouse inside, with a flagstone floor and a white deal table in the enormous, kitchen-like bar-parlour, and clean sawdust every day in the Jubilee spittoons.

('A free pint if you cop the Queen in the eye,' says Chunker Wilson.)

The boys return to school. The sun swings and sinks. Shadows merge into the snow; the woodcut turns into a shadowy chalk drawing. And the elder Miss Snoot at her window high up in Old Odborough looks over the roofs of the town.

It is early evening. Snow and cloud are in collusion and the town is more of a memory than a view. It is impossible to tell which is earth and which is sky, though eastward what looks like a whiter than usual cloud must surely be snow on the fells of Furness. Nearer, a blur of smoke and mist is simmering up from the snow, among all the spikiness of spire and steeple, chimney-stack and telegraph pole, the pinnacles of chapels and ventilators of schools. The houses of Old Odborough are already lighting up for the evening, but it is not yet dark enough to see the lights farther away.

Miss Snoot will be glad when it is dark. She hates Odborough and does not want to see more of it than need be. When her father retired she and her sisters begged him to take a bungalow up the coast, but he insisted on remaining in Odborough, choosing this house from where he can see, half a mile away, the roof and chimney of the shop where he made his money.

He is sitting there now, fat and inanimate as a sack of flour, staring out of the window as the lights come on. Soon the blurred sketch of the view will disappear and in its place will come an entanglement of lights. It is old Mr Snoot's ambition to learn to recognise every one of them. As the years go on he is gradually charting his universe, plotting each constellation and learning the names of every major star. Straight ahead is what he calls Orion, the three lights of the furnace top making the belt. Away to the south-west, well clear of the town, is the Plough or Great Bear—six or seven distant lights scattered among the farms around Oatrigg. To the east, the lights of Beckside Station, across the estuary, make the Little Bear. And running diagonally across his star-map is the Milky Way—the cream and dazzle of lights that stretch from the goods-yard down the Ironworks sidings, along the foot of the slag-bank, to the Ironworks themselves.

But it is no longer these stars of the first magnitude that hold his fancy. It is the lesser lights, the little twinkles from alley and shop or upstairs window that no one but himself could attempt to identify. It fills him with strange satisfaction to think that while the great illumination of the Market Square is quite invisible from this point, the little lamps of Iron Green can be seen glowing through a gap beyond Albert Road. It is many years now since he has visited the lower end of Odborough, for his legs will not carry him up and down the hill, and he growls like a dog if anyone suggests a car. But the sight of a street-lamp or a window light that he can recognise hooks up memories like fish from a pool. Then the night glows with an illuminated slide of *The Crown* Green, and the naphtha flares round the hobby horses, and Happy Homes Ltd, where he served his apprenticeship, bright as Jupiter in an extravagance of gas.

It is immensely difficult to identify these smaller lights. He will fix his eyes on some spot that he thinks he knows and watch it intently as the day fades, hoping to be able to plot any light that may appear later on. The view is always dimmed out, however, before the light declares itself, and there is a period of blurred dark when perspective shuts up like a concertina and the eye loses its bearings. It would be easier, he thinks, at dawn, to fix his gaze steadily on one particular light and then to establish its place in the returning landscape. But his daughters, on whom he is as dependent as a baby, refuse to get up in what they call the middle of the night to enable him to pursue his observations.

He glances towards Oatrigg, lifting his eyes to the other sky. Venus is powerful, in spite of the ground mist. It strikes him suddenly that Venus is in the wrong place. She does not belong in that unpeopled swash of sunset above the dunes and the sea. She belongs, surely, where he had seen her a thousand times as he came out of Happy Homes, just above the end pinnacle of the Wesleyan Methodist Chapel. Perhaps on a hundredth of those thousand times, seeing her there, it had moved him to think how in so many towns like Odborough men were looking up at her as they shut shops or walked home from mills and mines. And he would think how to each of them she had her proper place, to the left of the Town Clock or to the right of the water-tower—one single, certain planet shining across all the roofs of England.

He returns to his routine, but finds that once again he has failed. While his thoughts were on Venus the landscape was rubbed away like chalk from a blackboard and he has lost the means of identifying the newly discovered stars. . . .

Miss Snoot moves as if to draw the curtains, but her father forbids her with a shake of his head. Not that he wants to look out of the window any longer. Instead, his mind is on the great frosts of his youth, when the snow lay so deep on *The Crown* Green that they had to dig a trench to the shop door. When the railway and the two roads were blocked with drifts, and not a train or a letter or a newspaper came to the town for a week. When old Aaron Tyson from Limestone Hill sold to the greengrocer's the turnips he'd stacked up for his sheep. When women went on their knees to Absalom Dale, of Cheap and Best, for a handful of yeast. When the Dunner froze at low tide and you could skate from Odborough to Furness. When it was so cold in the winding shed at the mines that the men begged to go down the pit to get warm.

He revels in the memory of it, making it froth and lather all round the alleys and back-yards of youth very nearly up to the roof-tops. It is a sign you are growing old when you do not enjoy the snow. But when you are indeed old, then you can enjoy it again. He does not have to worry any longer about the slither and the slush.

'Let it snow till it reaches the chimney-pots,' he says to himself.

Let it snow up to the Market Clock. Let the snow heap itself high as the slag-bank, high as the furnace chimneys, high as St Kentigern's steeple. In a warm blizzard of drowsiness he watches the snow sud and curdle over the roofs and spires of the New Town, mounting up the slope of Old Odborough, up the hill of the Main Street, till it reaches Mount Pleasant. And when at last it drifts through the window and fluffs all round his feet and legs, even then he does not let himself be disturbed.

I2

Playing on the Lake-Shore

ARTHUR RANSOME

*Arthur Ransome had an extraordinary life. His long association
with the* Manchester Guardian *provided him with opportunities
to be where history was being formed. He witnessed the Russian
Revolution in 1917, for example. (And, as no logical consequence,
it can be added that he married Trotsky's secretary.) But it is as
the author of children's books—particularly* Swallows and
Amazons—*that he is remembered. When his autobiography was
published in 1976 (nine years after his death) it was possible to
see how his own childhood had sown the ground for those later
stories.*

I was a disappointment to my father in many ways, but
shared to the full his passion for the hills and lakes of Furness.
He had been born on the shores of Morecambe Bay within
sight of the hills, held himself an exile when in Leeds and,
to make up as far as he could for his eldest son's being born
in a town, carried me up to the top of Coniston Old Man
at such an early age that I think no younger human being
can ever have been there. Leeds in those days was a good
place for a country-bred professor. My father fished or shot
every week-end while he lived there. This was in term-time
when he was lecturing five days a week, and busy in the
evenings with his working men's club, his Conversation
Club and with the ground-work of his history-books. The
moment term was over he was off to the North taking his
family with him. Every Long Vacation he was no longer a

professor who fished, but a fisherman who wrote history-books in his spare time.

Preparations began long before the end of term. There would be an orgy of fly-tying. My father tied for his friends and for himself the delicate Yorkshire wet flies that T. E. Pritt pictured in his famous book, lightly hackled and dressed on short lengths of fine gut or horsehair. My father was one of the first to introduce Halford's methods in the North and to fish with dry fly, but after a year or so he gave up tying dry flies because he had no time to spare for them and he was himself first of all a wet-fly trout-fisher. Long before the day of the journey the wooden candlesticks in his study were festooned with new-made casts, his rods were ready, his landing-net mended, an inspection held of our perch-floats, and our shotted casts for perch-fishing hung beside his own. Meanwhile my mother was busy day after day patching and mending our clothes, replacing used half-pans of water-colour (she used to run short of cobalt blue) and buying (we used to remind her) sheets of transfers to keep us happy on the rainy days that we knew, in the Lake District, to be inevitable. A huge supply of ginger-nuts was bought for the train journey. At last came the great moment of Sitting on the Bath. The bath was a large, deep, tin one, painted a mottled orange-brown. It had a flat lid, a staple, a padlock and a huge leather strap over all. The bath, used at Christmas for a bran-pie, stuffed with presents, with a cotton-wool crust that was cut with a monster paper-knife, was now crammed with bedding and clothes that filled it and rose high above it. The lid was pressed down on the top and my mother began to wonder what could be left out. We children climbed on and slid off and climbed again. With the weight of all of us together the lid sank but never far enough. The end of the strap (which at first would not reach so far) was put through its buckle, and mother and nurse gained on it, one hole at a time. Still blankets, sheets and underclothes oozed from beneath it and we went officiously about it and about, poking them back. Then, when we had done our utmost one of us was sent down for the cook, a big, cheerful, brawny Armstrong from Northumberland who allowed us in the kitchen but once a year, to wish while we stirred her Christmas pudding with a long-handled spoon, her own huge hands engulfing our small ones and providing the force to drive the spoon round and round through the stiff, currant-spotted mass of uncooked pudding. The cook would wipe her vast forearms, come up to the nursery, laugh at the sight of us waiting, defeated, round the bath, seat herself solidly on the lid and another half-dozen holes were gained in a moment. But even with the weight of Molly Armstrong I can never remember the lid closing far enough to let my mother use the padlock. 'It'll have to do now,' she would say, and that was that.

Then next day there was a hurried run round to say fare-well to the hole in the grubby evergreens (Leeds was a smoky city) that only we knew was a robbers' cave. Then came the drive down into Leeds in an old four-wheeled cab, the bulk of the luggage having gone before. The railway journey through the outskirts of Leeds, through smoky Holbeck, past the level crossing that we knew from our 'walks', and on by Wharfedale to Hellifield, my father's gun and rods on the rack, ginger-nuts crunching in our mouths, noses pressed to the windows to watch the dizzying rise and fall of the telegraph wires beside the track, was a long-drawn-out ecstasy, and not for children alone. By the time we reached Arkholme we could feel my father's mounting excitement (he had been pointing out to us one by one the rivers we crossed). At Carnforth we had to change from one train to another unless, as in later years, my father had been able to book an entire 'saloon' carriage for us and our luggage, so that we could sit in it until it was coupled to the other train, on the Furness Railway that we always counted as peculiarly our own. There were well-known landmarks as the train ran slowly round Morecambe Bay. There was the farmhouse that was built like a little fortress against raiding Scots. There was Arnside Tower. There were our own Lake hills, and Coniston Old Man with a profile very different from the lofty cone it showed to us at Nibthwaite. Then at last we were at Greenodd, where the Crake and the Leven poured together to the sea not a stone's throw from the rail-way line. There would be John Swainson from Nibthwaite, or Edward his son, with a red farm-cart and a well-beloved young lad with a wagonette. We climbed, or were lifted, down to the platform to be greeted by my father's old friend, the station-master, with the latest news of the two rivers. We watched the train go on without us across the bridge and away up the valley of the Leven. Anxiously we watched the loading of the cart, holding our breaths lest the bath should burst its strap before being roped down on the top of all. Then came the slow drive up the valley of the Crake, always halting at the Thurstonville Lodge for a word with the keeper there. Up the winding hill and down again by Lowick Green, over the river at Lowick Bridge, where my father had a look at that streamy water just below, as I have so often had a look sixty years later. We stopped again by a little wooden bridge close to one of my father's favourite places, and again by the Hart Jacksons' cottage, had a glimpse of Allan Tarn, rumbled over Nibthwaite Beck at the entrance to the tiny village, turned to the right up the road to Bethecar, a steep short pull between barn and orchard, for which we all got out, and there we were at the farm, being greeted by Mrs Swainson and her daughters, and getting our first proper sight of the lake itself—Coniston Water.

Tea was always ready for our arrival, and after the long journey we were always made to get that meal over before doing anything else. Then 'May I get down?' and we were free in paradise, sniffing remembered smells as we ran about making sure that familiar things were still in their places. I used first of all to race down to the lake, to the old stone harbour to which, before the Furness Railway built its branch line to Coniston village, boats used to bring their cargoes of copper-ore from the mines on the Old Man. The harbour was a rough stone-built dock, with an old shed or two, and beside it was a shallow cut, perhaps six feet across and twenty long, where the Swainsons' boat, *our* boat, was pulled up half way out of the shallow, clear water which always seemed alive with minnows. I had a private rite to perform. Without letting the others know what I was doing, I had to dip my hand in the water, as a greeting to the beloved lake or as a proof to myself that I had indeed come home. In later years, even as an old man, I have laughed at myself, resolved not to do it, and every time have done it again. If I were able to go back there today, I should feel some discomfort until after coming to the shore of the lake I had felt its coolness on my fingers.

After the solemn secret touching of the lake I had to make sure that other things were as they had been. I used to race back to the farmhouse, to find my father already gone with a rod to the river, my mother and our nurse busy unpacking, and (though the younger ones might be detained) nothing wanted from me except to keep out of the way. I had to make sure that the butter-churn was in its old place, and the grandfather clock in the kitchen still whirring wheezily as it struck the hours. I had to glance into the earth closet in the garden, with its three sociable seats, two for grown-ups and one small one for a baby in the middle, to see that there had been no changes in the decoration of its walls. These were papered with pages from *Punch* bearing the mystic word 'charivari' and with pictures from the *Illustrated London News*, including portraits of Mr Gladstone, of whom (after the affair of the yellow ribbon) I was an obstinate supporter. The newspapers, no doubt, had been left by other visitors, and the pictures showing Conservatives and Liberals alike impartially pasted up by the farmer.

Then I had to have a look at the cowsheds, and the hayloft above them, the blue and red haycart, the damson orchard, and from a safe distance the bee-hives and the muckheap in the farmyard that had a top that looked solid but was not, as I had learnt by jumping down on it from the orchard wall. From there it was only a few steps to the beck, and I had to make sure that I could still crawl through under the bridge. Then up to the farm again and through the gate behind it. Through that gate went the rough fell-road to Bethecar and Parkamoor, winding and climbing through a wild country of rock and sheep-cropped grass, purple heather and bracken (much less then than now). Here was the Knickerbockerbreaker, a smooth precipitous rock easy to climb from one side for the pleasure of sliding down its face to the damage of my knickerbockers which, when they were threadbare, kind Annie Swainson used to darn *in situ*. Sharp to the right through the gate a grass track led up the steep sides of Brockbarrow (Badger Hill) and not far up that track was a group of rocks making something like a boat. This we called the Gondola. Seated in it, we could look out high above the lake to the pier on the further side at which the real Gondola called, giving a warning whistle just before it came

into view round the trees on the Waterpark promontory.
This was a steam vessel, shaped like an Italian gondola, with
a serpent figurehead, formally approved by Mr Ruskin who
lived at Brantwood and, a legendary figure, was sometimes
to be seen slipping furtively off the road, taking refuge behind
a tree from the very few strangers who walked along it.

Those holidays at Nibthwaite I owe to my father's passion
for the lake country. They bred a similar passion in me that
has lasted my life and been the mainspring of the books I
have been happiest in writing. Always that country has been
'home', and smoky old Leeds, though well beloved, was
never as real as Swainson's farm, Coniston lake and the valley
of the Crake. There, in the heavy farm boat, with its oars
that worked on pins instead of in rowlocks (so that a fisherman could drop them instantly if a pike or a char took his
trailed spinner) I learned to be at home on the water. My
father had rowed at Oxford and from the beginning taught
his children to row with their backs and to regard their arms
merely as strings connecting the oars to the part that did the
pulling. 'In ... Out! What are you doing with those elbows?
... Keep your eyes on stroke's shoulders ... Now then ...
Ten strokes both together ... In! ... Out! ... In! ... Out! ...
(Crash!) You again, Arthur!' My feet had slipped off the
stretcher or my oar had missed the water and I was on my
back with my feet in the air. 'Nothing to howl about. That's
catching a crab. Better men than you have caught them
before now ... But not two in one day ... Up you get. Go
on now. In! ... Out! ... In! ... Out! Easy all!'

There was no end to the pleasures of Nibthwaite. We
made friends with the farm animals, with the charcoal-
burners who in those days still dwelt in wigwams carefully
watching their smoking mounds, with the postman, several
gamekeepers, several poachers and various fishermen. We
took part in the haymaking, turned the butter-churn for
Annie Swainson, picked mushrooms and blackberries,
tickled trout under the little bridge, went for rare educative
walks with my father who, like my grandfather, was a first-
rate ornithologist and naturalist (though neither he nor my
mother was good on the names of wild flowers). That road
along the east side of Coniston lake, now dangerous with
motor traffic, was then very little used. I came once upon a

red squirrel, rolled up in a ball, fast asleep on a sunny patch in the middle of the road, picked it up to put it in safety and was well bitten for my pains. I also came upon a wounded heron and, knowing no better, took it in my arms and carried it back to Nibthwaite, looking for first aid. I was lucky not to lose an eye. The heron kept stabbing with its long bill, and I suppose I escaped only because I was holding my patient so tight in my arms that with its head at my shoulder it could not reach my face.

We used to catch minnows in the little cut where the Swainsons kept their boat, and we were taken perch-fishing, each of us watching a float of a different colour. This, of course, was very different from merely watching someone else catch fish. Then too, sometimes, when my father was fishing the lake for trout he would row his whole family up to Peel Island where we landed in the lovely little harbour at the south end (that some who have read my books as children may recognise borrowed for the sake of secrecy to improve an island in another lake). We spent the day as savages. My mother would settle down to make a sketch in water-colours. My father, forgetting to eat his sandwiches, would drift far along the lake-shores, casting his flies and coming back in the evening with trout in the bottom of the boat for Mrs Swainson to cook for next day's breakfast. . . .

We all knew that though, at Nibthwaite, we were on holiday, my father was hard at work. On wet days this was difficult for him with his children (in the end there were four of us) busy at the table with saucers of water, sheets of paper and transfers. He consequently had to work on many days when he should have been out of doors. His rod stood ready, leaning against the porch and, on likely days, it was our business, playing by the boat-landing (well out of hearing from the house), to watch for the time of the rise. Close to that landing is the place where the river Crake leaves the lake and here in the shallowish water on a calm day, the first signs were to be seen. The water would be as still as glass and then, suddenly, one of us would see rings spreading where a trout had come up and dimpled the surface in taking a fly. One such rise meant nothing. We waited, watching, and if the first was followed by another and then another, we would race off with the news, burst breathless but welcome

into the farmhouse parlour where my father sat at work, and
he, knowing that if the fish were rising there they would be
rising in the river, would leave his papers, take his rod and
hurry across the fields to the Crake. Hard worker as he was,
he did not waste good fishing-weather on writing history-
books. It was on the windless days when the lake was useless
that we had to watch for rises while he stayed in the farm to
write.

He enjoyed Nibthwaite as much as any of us. He used to
shoot grouse and blackcock on the high fells and we used,
as beaters, to struggle through the heather and come down
through a big larch wood to the lake-shore where, fifty
years later, I was to have a cottage. He used to get sea-trout
from the Crake, and I can still hear the sudden scream of his
reel when, wading in the pool below the bobbin-mill, he
hooked a big mort while my mother was sketching on the
bank and I was looking at the seething, squirming mass of
eels in the eel-coop by the mill.

He enjoyed spinning for pike in Allan Tarn and on the
lake and used to put a spaniel ashore, and whistling to it as he
drifted along would bring it splashing through the reeds to
drive the pike out of their fastnesses into the open water,
where they could see his artificial baits, made by himself
and painted realistically by my mother. I remember being
with him in the boat and rowing when he hooked a very
big pike, some twenty pounds, just off the point by Brown
How (where there was a kingfisher's nest in a hole in the
rock, with a pile of little fish-bones below it). The pike went
off at a great pace, pulling the boat after it, so that my father
had no chance of making sure it was properly hooked. 'Back-
water, you little idiot!' I can hear my father exclaim as,
violently rowing, I pulled after the pike instead of holding
water, back-watering and making the boat go the other way.
However, in spite of my inefficiency, he got that pike and a
very good one it was.

With the end of each Long Vacation we had to leave
Nibthwaite and go back to Leeds. We stayed to the last
possible day in deepening melancholy. The Gondola did not
run during the winter and old Captain Hamill (who let me,
as a very small boy, steer his noble vessel, standing behind
me at the wheel on the top of the long cabin) performed a

rite of his own. When for the last time in the year the Gondola left the pier that we could see from the farmhouse windows, he used to sound his whistle, a long last wail of farewell until he was out of sight. It always rained on that day, both indoors and out of doors. The rain would stream down the window outside, and we with our noses pressed against the glass were blinded by our tears.

★   ★   ★

1929 was for me the year of crisis, a hinge year as it were, joining and dividing two quite different lives. It was the year in which, at last, I felt myself released from the obligation to go on with the work that had come to me with the war. Feeling free from that obligation I seem to have run amuck with liberty. To refuse a career offered by the *Manchester Guardian* must have seemed to C. P. Scott something very like sacrilege. Ted Scott, on the other hand, knew that I had never given up the hope that sooner or later I should get back to writing books, and he was too good a friend not to understand and to astonish his father by showing that he understood why, instead of welcoming the opportunity of becoming a full-time employee of the paper, I saw his offer as a warning and felt that once in the Corridor I should never be able to escape.

Ted told his father that my real interest was in books, not politics; but it was political articles that C.P.S. wanted from me. Finally C.P.S. told me that he planned for me eventually to succeed Monkhouse as literary editor, but that meanwhile I was to go to Berlin as resident correspondent. This was exactly what I wished to avoid. It was one thing to get a telegram asking for a leading article on some subject I was supposed to know something about. It would be quite another thing to be tied to a newspaper office. I told him I did not know German. He said that, after Russian, I should find German easy. On March 2 I lunched with him and he proposed a salary that seemed to me enormous. I went home to share a decision that would affect my wife as much as myself, and we foresaw that if I were to accept that offer I should once again be hopelessly involved in controversial politics, which of all things I most loathed, and that, if I were again to become so involved, I should never be able to get out. By March 19 Evgenia and I had made up our minds and I gave three months' notice to the *Manchester Guardian*, ending the existing arrangement, as I was sure I should not be able to do what was wanted in Berlin. On March 24, after a couple of days' sailing, with a weight off my shoulders but with no prospects whatever, I began the writing of *Swallows and Amazons*.

I had for some time been growing intimate with a family of imaginary children. I had even sketched out the story of two boats in which my four (five including the baby) were to meet another two, Nancy and Peggy, who had sprung to life one day when, sailing on Coniston, I had seen two girls playing on the lake-shore. For once I had without difficulty shaped the tale into scenes and even found the chapter-headings. The whole book was clear in my head. I had only to write it, but dreaded the discovery that after all these years of writing discursively I was unable to write narrative. I well remember the pleasure I had in the first chapter, and my fear that it would also be the last. I could think of nothing else and grudged every moment that had to be given to other activities. I wrote on plain paper with holes along one edge, so that the sheets could be clipped into a loose-leaf quarto binding. Night after night I used to bring it in a small attaché case from my workroom in the old barn to the cottage, so that I could reach out and lay my hand on it in the dark beside my bed. When I had fifty pages in that loose cover I felt I had gone so far with it that this time I should be able to write the whole story. I decided to take the risk of offering it to a publisher. If he seemed willing, I would go on. If not, delightful as was the prospect of writing it, I should feel that I must work on at that other writing for which I knew I had a market. We were too poor to take a greater risk.

Jonathan Cape, whom I had met years before, and now met again at Molly Hamilton's, had seen the weekly articles that I was writing for the *Guardian* and made a remark that was prophetic in a way he did not expect. What he said was: 'Isn't it time that you were putting together some books to support you when you grow old?' What he proposed was that I should collect a volume of essays for him, and then another, until he had published a series of them. I went up to town in April, taking with me the typescript of *Rod and Line*, a selection from my fishing papers which I hoped I could persuade him to accept as the first of my volumes of essays. I also took with me on half a sheet of notepaper the title and a list of the chapter-headings of *Swallows and Amazons*. I did not want to show him any of the first draft of the book if I could help it, though I had shown some of it to Molly Hamilton and been enormously encouraged by her liking it.

Cape agreed at once that *Rod and Line* should count as the first of the volumes of essays, but said that what he really wanted was a collection of such essays on general subjects. With some diffidence I told him about *Swallows and Amazons* and showed him my half-sheet of paper. He glanced at it. 'That's all right,' said Napoleon Cape. 'We'll publish it and pay one hundred pounds in advance on account of royalties. But it's the essays we want.'

13
Wood Fires
JOHN WYATT

'The Story of a Man Who Went Back to Nature' is how John Wyatt subtitles his autobiography. In one sense it's part of every man's dream at some time or other—to make for the country and live off and in nature. Wyatt made a job of it and is now Head Warden of the Lake District National Park. Here he describes his early home when he came 'back to Nature'.

What I shall always remember most about the hut is the large wood-burning fireplace—and the smoke. The chimney was a traditional one for the Lake District; a straight, dry-stone cylinder tapering slightly inside as it went up. If you sat in the fireplace and looked up you could see a disc of sky and several iron hooks in silhouette. The structure was fine if you wanted to smoke hams or fish, or season walking-sticks; as an accessory to a heat producer it was a failure. If there was the slightest breeze from any direction the smoke would spread itself evenly between chimney and room in more or less equal proportions, which was why the once white walls had the appearance of very old ivory and the mounted fox heads, hunting trophies which hung on the walls, had a fine coating of brown dust, and their yellow eyes a slightly inebriated, glazed expression. The smell of the place reminded me of a kipper factory. I was soon thoroughly cured, inside and out!

At first the wood smoke brought distressing symptoms of choking and crying, and I was continually opening windows and doors—with little apparent effect except to sweep in cold draughts which swirled the smoke around. But after a week or so I was acclimatised, and I would laugh at the discomforts of half-asphyxiated visitors. Strangely, though, the symptoms returned to me every night when I retired to my bunk which occupied a corner of the same room. I cried like a baby every time I tried to close my eyes. All my possessions began to smell of smoke; even my better clothes which I kept in a closed cupboard under the bunk.

I soon became a connoisseur of wood smoke. For fragrance, in my opinion, there is little to match juniper; I would stack this wood aside against the days I had visitors. Apple and well-seasoned cherry are pure luxury too. Holly and birch have a clean tang. Ash, particularly green ash, smells like washing day. Old oak has an honest, pungent, lusty smell as you would expect. The other hardwoods are hardly worth a mention smokewise. The soft woods; pine, spruce or larch are rather vulgar; but there is something to be said for a really old vintage larch root.

Once one gets the taste for smoking wood it is possible to mix and obtain subtle flavours; and invent recipes. Prepare a fire base of larch kindling; add well-seasoned oak until the logs redden deeply; place one large back-log of holly, and add, from the fire back to the front, one crab-apple log, one of well-dried cherry and one of birch. An ideal after-dinner mixture....

My daily routine began with wood-cutting for fuel. There is, of course, a mystique about wood-burning. Some have romantic visions of crouched and muffled figures dragging log-laden sledges through a savage landscape of snow and ice; frost-bearded Vikings with massive axes, round great fires of pine logs; or raw-boned Northerners squatting over faggot-heated porridge pots. Many town-dwellers burn wood for pleasure. One man I know did very well once out of selling 'yule logs' by post. His romantic northern-sounding address, evocative of resinous forest smells and ice-wracked lakes, helped his business more than a little. His customers were not buying fuel but the magic of dreams and memories of childhood story books.

All wood-burning pundits have their prejudices and the commonest one is against elm. It will not burn, they say; or it 'burns cold'. Only wych elm grew in the wood and it burned for me quite well when dry. For common elm I cannot speak, but the age-old superstition that elm 'loveth not mankind' persists. Does it not, without warning, drop its boughs? It does. And is it not the best wood for coffins? It is. Yet I knew a Wiltshire man who said that he burned hardly anything else; and it was very fine, he said, when well seasoned.

Ash is the darling of the wood burners. It cuts well, and splits beautifully, and burns even when it is green; and it is a fast grower. Alder burns well, dry; but if you use it exclusively you will be sawing all day. Sycamore and birch, too, burn fast; so for long-lasting stuff you need oak, beech and, best of all, hawthorn: all splendid when well seasoned. But holly logs are in a class of their own. Yew, too—but this wood is like iron and will break or blunt your axe, your saw, and your spirit. Of the soft woods pine is good, and larch as well if you are in a hurry for a blaze and prepared to roll back the hearth-rug in preparation for the spectacular fusillade.

Wood-burning is so aesthetically pleasing. Every log, as it is picked up, can be examined as an individual work of art—shape, grain, colour, weight—before being placed carefully on the fire in the correct position, to give its own artistic display of pyrotechnics. And in an idle moment by the fire's warmth you can take a knife and improve on the art of nature, carving into the wood, or cutting designs into the bark. Or you can play building and balancing games.

I had to gather kindling too, for storing in a dry place. Larch and pine logs could be split small and dried by the fire; or kindling could be gathered 'raw'. Holly again would be my first choice. The thin dead twigs from a holly tree will start a fire even if gathered wet and then merely shaken. But hollies are rather miserly with their dead twigs, and the only worthy substitute, with a generous yield, is birch. I have won several bets in my time from workmates, by starting a fire outdoors, in heavy rain, without the use of any dry medium such as paper. The trick is easy if there are birch trees about; then there is always an abundance of dead twigs which can be snapped easily off the trunks. From these can be gathered a handful of needle-thin stuff that can be pushed into a pocket while you collect slightly thicker material. A good pile is made of the birch twigs; then, when all is ready, the handful of needle-thins is taken from the pocket (where they have left much of their moisture), put into the fire centre, and carefully lit with a match. The wood contains sufficient natural oil to start the fire well.

Once kindled, stoking the fire can be a work of art. A large back-log is necessary; it should be heavy hardwood—fresh-cut green stuff will do at a pinch—and this acts as a reflector. Holly is the best, and a good log will burn for two days; a really good green one will last for several days. The morning fire should be re-kindled from the back-log of the previous day: a smart blow with the poker to break off its embers, small kindling on top of these, a puff with the bellows or breath and she is away.

14

After the Fair

MELVYN BRAGG

In Norman Nicholson's Lake District anthology, he is sensibly clear-headed about including his own work where he thinks it is useful. Following that excellent precedent, I include a passage from The Hired Man, *a novel set in Cumbria from 1898–1923. Here the young hired man, John, eighteen, having walked thirty miles to get employment, has been landed with a poor place and low wages. He has met his brothers at the fair which accompanies the hiring but otherwise there has been no joy; certainly nothing to bring to his wife, Emily, who has been driven up to the town and found refuge in the house of a local schoolmaster, Mr Stephens.*

When Mr Stephens went out to buy more provisions for tea —though his excuse offered was that he needed some tobacco—John sat in a chair on one side of the kitchen, Emily stood by the window on the other side, both on their best behaviour. But while he was most conscious of himself, clumsy in uneasy gratitude, Emily was delighted with it all. After seeing Mr Stephens disappear around the corner, she examined the small room minutely, the books on the shelf— reading out all their titles aloud—the three prints on the wall, 'The Education of the Young Raleigh', 'Derwentwater at Dawn' and 'The Drunkard's Children'—drew her boots appreciatively over the mat, picked up the jug of pencils and finally came to the oven which was next to the sink. Above the sink was a large cupboard which she opened despite the disapproving suck of John's tongue.

'I could make some biscuits,' she said. 'Do you think I should?'

'Leave things be, Emily,' John replied, speaking softly in the new place. 'Thou can't go using other people's stuff like that.'

'He would like some biscuits.'

'How dis' thou know?'

'He would.' She shut one of the cupboard doors only, not to be defeated that easily, and then thought of a conclusive argument. 'I bet he can't make them himself!'

'Well, what's that got to do with it?'

'A lot.' But she swung the second door in her hand uncertainly. 'Don't you think he would like some?'

'How do I know?'

'There you are!' She smiled. 'You can't be certain. It'll be done in a minute.'

'He won't want his kitchen mired up wid baking stuffs. That I do know.'

'And who'll mire a kitchen up?'

'Thou's bound to.'

'I am not, John Tallentire! And anyway, it's clean dirt. It's easily mopped up.' She paused. 'He would like some,' she reiterated. 'I could make ginger snaps. He has some ginger.'

'Do as you please.'

'Wouldn't you like a ginger snap?'

'O, for pity's sake Emily, stop keeping on!'

She slammed the door shut and went back to the window. She glanced at John quickly and then leaned forward, slipped the latch, and pushed it open. Through the rain came the sound of the fair, organ music squeezing enticingly away, unseen.

'So I won't get to the fair,' said Emily—and then, the second she had said it, she covered her mouth with her hand, afraid that her thoughtlessness might upset John. And so before he could say a word, she rushed on. 'Still! I've been to Cockermouth in a pony and trap!'

John got up and went across to her. She heard him but kept her back turned so that she would have his arms around her and then she could wriggle inside them to face him. As he held her she seemed to swell, as if another skin, another body, more calm and perfect than the one she had, grew out

of her as token for that love of him which could in looks
and words show itself so inadequately. He kissed her on
the cheek and her eyes closed to feel his lips breathing so
tenderly.

'I'm sorry about the fair,' he said.

'Don't be sorry.'

'We'll come next year.'

'Yes.'

He released her, held her on the shoulders for a moment
and quickly turned away.

'There were some logs in his backyard,' he said. 'I'll chop
them up for kindling.' Use the axe to cut out the feeling of
obligation.

'O! That's good!'

'Emily,' he asked as he reached the door. 'Twelve shillin's
will be enough, won't it?'

'Plenty!' she answered. 'And if you can chop wood, I can
make biscuits.'

By the time Mr Stephens came back, the snaps were almost
done, the table was laid, crockery out, a split log burned on
the fire, there was a neat pile of sticks drying in the grate,
and tea went well. They talked of the market and the fair,
and then, Emily having noticed and praised his drawings of
the swans, Mr Stephens held forth about his hobby.

'What d'you call a missel thrush down your way?' he
asked John. 'Is it a shalary?'

'Yes. That's right. There is a shalary.'

'I thought so,' said Mr Stephens, happily. 'Even in our
county it changes its name all over the place. There's storm-
cock and chur-cock and shell-cock, shalary and mountain
throssel—all the missel thrush!'

'There's something my grandfather calls a shrike,' said
John, 'would that be another?'

'It might be. It might be! I'll ask Mr Carrick tomorrow.
Shrike! I'll make a note of that.'

'There's something I call a blue-wing,' said Emily, boldly,
pleased to be joining in a conversation in which she was
proud to see John taking such an active part, 'and my uncle
Tom calls it a blue-back.'

'That's the "field-fare",' said Mr Stephens. 'Turdus pilaris.'
And the Latin appellation—memorized so painstakingly—

crunched between his teeth like barley sugar. 'Your grandfather might have heard it called the felty, or the pigeon felty
or even the blue felty—and I think some call it fell fo!'

'Goodness!' said Emily, mouth half-open.

'Oh, that's just the beginning!' Mr Stephens responded.
'Now take the whitethroat—sylvia cinerea   ...'

But after the tea had been cleared, the cups put away, everything tidied, then the three of them sat around in broken
sentences. Because of the regular placement of the chairs
around the fire, they were quite close together—and yet the
small spaces between them quickly became boundaries. John
wanted to be in bed so that the night would be over quickly
and he could move off the next morning; Mr Stephens had
a neighbour who would lend them a handcart and John
wanted to be able to push the furniture the eight miles uphill
to Crossbridge, settle it, and return the handcart the same
day. Already he was worried about their stores lasting until
the Saturday when he might reasonably claim a few shillings
to tide him over; Emily's mother had given them a box of
stuff, sausages, bread, some tea, butter, bacon—but it would
have to be spun out. He was burrowing into responsibilities,
looking for them almost, for they gave substance to that
which bound Emily to him—and still the shock of jealousy
pulsed occasionally making him shudder so that he blushed to
seem to be shivering.

The schoolteacher realized that his guests were tongue-tied
in this strange place and, after a few openings had brought
no more than murmurs of self-conscious or self-absorbed
politeness, he did what he had found best to do on such
occasions. For he was not a man who could slither into any
shape required of him. His interests and habits had been too
strictly and personally framed for him to be anything less
than completely reliant on them. So he did what he was
going to do anyway, what would most engage his own
attention, and invited the others to share the preoccupation—
which was as much as any man could do, he thought.

He took down a copy of Wordsworth's collected poems.
John and Emily sat themselves up to listen, and felt most
solemn: but the schoolmaster's plain reading gave them confidence and Emily's hand reached out to touch John's arm.

Mr Stephens was careful to read the short poems and finished up with one set not far from the place at which John was hired. Beginning:

> 'There is a yew-tree, pride of Lorton Vale,
>   Which to this day stands single, in the midst
>   Of its own darkness, as it stood of yore.'

And John felt Emily's hand tighten on his own as the last lines rolled out:

> '... beneath whose sable roof
> Of boughs, as if for festal purpose decked
> With unrejoicing berries—ghostly shapes
> May meet at noon-tide; Fear and trembling Hope,
> Silence and Foresight; Death the skeleton
> And Time the Shadow:—there to celebrate,
> As in a natural temple scattered o'er
> With altars undisturbed of mossy stone
> United Worship; or in mute repose
> To lie, and listen to the mountain flood
> Murmuring from Glaramara's inmost caves.'

That final line itself murmured through the kitchen and they sat silently, the organ music from the streets like the sound from the caves. John looked at Emily and saw a face on which such a keen reverence was trying to settle itself to gaze of understanding that yet again he stirred against the schoolmaster. He had no such means of casting spells over her. They came from a world out of reach. And he did not want to hear of what was impossible.

When the couple had gone upstairs to bed, Mr Stephens packed his bag for the next day's outing, bolted the doors firmly—for many of the men stayed in Cockermouth drinking for three or four days and would roam the streets at night looking for somewhere to sleep—and then, as if to atone for those first designs he had had on Emily, he picked out *Silas Marner* from his bookshelf and wrapped it up as a present for her. He pushed back the chairs and laid his blankets on the floor to fall asleep, as always, the moment he closed his eyes.

John could not sleep. He had stayed in bed until Emily was settled and then, very quietly, got up. The window in the bedroom was very small and all he could see through it were the roof-tops lit, as the previous night, by a full moon.

He could not recapture the certainty he had felt that morning. And it was not only that he had not got what he had hoped for, nor was it the jealousy which made him feel unsure. In The Ring his pride in being on his own had met with confusion and Isaac and Seth, too, seemed to challenge what he wanted, what he believed in, how he lived—though understandingly enough, he knew. It was as if he had caught an infection which was moving around all men but as yet lighting on few, something which would grow to cause fever where there had been force. He shook his head, abruptly. No wonder you get like that, standing in your bare feet in the middle of the night, his mother would have said. And he remembered Isaac's story about the man who thought too much and smiled once more.

Not until dawn, however, could he fall asleep. He lay in the bed, touching Emily with fingers too rough for her skin, wondering what he could give her that would even approach what he thought of her; waiting to be gone to his own place.

15
Notes in Conclusion
A. WAINWRIGHT

As Wordsworth had to open this compilation, so Wainwright must close it. The illustrated guides to fellwalking by this former borough treasurer from Kendal have brought the routes safely alive to thousands of tourists and locals alike. These 'notes in conclusion', written in 1965, are taken from the seventh, and last, book in his series A Pictorial Guide to the Lakeland Fells. *Since his retirement, mentioned at the end of this chapter, he has become Chairman of a charity, Animal Rescue, Cumbria, to care for creatures in distress; as he says, every true fellwalker develops a liking and compassion for birds and animals, often his only companions on a solitary walk. He has continued to explore the valleys and the fells and through his more recent books, such as* Fellwanderer, *to share with his readers his devotion to Lakeland. Between Wordsworth breathing the air of great literature and Wainwright firmly fixed on the ground, the place is well served.*

When I came down from Starling Dodd on the 10th of September 1965 I had just succeeded in obtaining a complete view from the summit before the mist descended, after laying patient siege to it through several wet weekends, and in so doing I had concluded the field work for my last book with only one week left before the end of the summer bus service put the fell out of reach. Thus a 13-year plan was finished one week ahead of schedule. Happy? Yes, I was happy, as anyone must be who comes to the end of a long road ahead of the clock. Sorry? Yes, I was sorry, as anyone must be who comes to the end of a long road he has enjoyed travelling. Relieved? Yes, I was relieved, because a broken leg during these years would have meant a broken heart, too.

I think I must concede that the scenery of the western half

of Lakeland (dropping a vertical through High Raise in the Central Fells) is, on the whole, better than the eastern, although it has nothing more beautiful than the head of Ullswater. This is not to say that the fellwalking is better: it is more exciting and exacting but the Helvellyn and High Street ranges in the east are supreme for the man who likes to stride out over the tops all day. Those who prefer to follow narrow ridges from summit to summit are best catered for in the west. The southern half, too, is generally finer than the northern, so that the highlights of the district are to be found mainly in the south-western sector, from the Duddon to Whinlatter. But it is all delectable country.... One advantage I found in roaming around the Western Fells is that they are still free from the type of visitor who has spoiled Langdale and Keswick and other places easier of access. Wasdale Head and Buttermere are beginning to suffer from tourist invasion, but on the tops one can still wander in solitude and enjoy the freedom characteristic of the whole district before somebody invented the motor car.

I promised to give my opinion of the six best fells. I should not have used the word 'best', which suggests that some are not as good as others. I think they are all good. The finest, however, must have the attributes of mountains, i.e., height, a commanding appearance, a good view, steepness and ruggedness: qualities that are most pronounced in the volcanic area of the south-western sector. I now give, after much biting of finger-nails, what I consider to be the finest half-dozen:

SCAFELL PIKE	GREAT GABLE
BOWFELL	BLENCATHRA
PILLAR	CRINKLE CRAGS

These are not necessarily the six fells I like best. It grieves me to have to omit Haystacks (most of all), Langdale Pikes, Place Fell, Carrock Fell and some others simply because they do not measure up in altitude to the grander mountains. There will be surprise at the omission of Scafell, the crags of which provide the finest sight in Lakeland, but too much of this fell is lacking in interest. It would be seventh if there were seven in the list. Contrary to general opinion (which would favour Great Gable), the grandest of the lot is Scafell Pike.

Of the six, all are of volcanic rock with the exception of Blencathra.

The six best summits (attributes: a small neat peak of naked rock with a good view) I consider to be

DOW CRAG, Coniston   EAGLE CRAG, Langstrath
HARTER FELL, Eskdale   SLIGHT SIDE, Scafell
HELM CRAG, Grasmere   STEEPLE, Ennerdale

All these, except Steeple, are accessible only by scrambling on rock. The top inches of Helm Crag are hardest to reach.

The six best places for a fellwalker to be (other than summits) because of their exciting situations, and which can be reached without danger, are

STRIDING EDGE, Helvellyn
First col. LORD'S RAKE, Scafell
MICKLEDORE, Scafell
SHARP EDGE, Blencathra
SOUTH TRAVERSE, Great Gable
SHAMROCK TRAVERSE, Pillar

Of course I haven't forgotten Jack's Rake on Pavey Ark. I never could. But this is a place only for men with hair on their chests. I am sorry to omit Great Slab and Climbers Traverse on Bowfell.

The finest ridge-walks are, I think,

THE FAIRFIELD HORSESHOE (Ambleside)
THE HIGH STREET RANGE (Garburn–Moor Divock)
THE MOSEDALE HORSESHOE (Wasdale Head)
CAUSEY PIKE–WHITELESS PIKE
GRISEDALE PIKE–WHITESIDE
ESK HAUSE–WRYNOSE PASS, via Bowfell
THE ESKDALE HORSESHOE (Slight Side–Bowfell)
THE HELVELLYN RANGE (Grisedale Pass–Threlkeld)
THE HIGH STILE RIDGE, with Haystacks
CATBELLS–DALE HEAD–HINDSCARTH–SCOPE END
THE CONISTON ROUND (Old Man–Wetherlam)
    (not in order of merit)

In my introductory remarks to Book One I described my task in compiling these books as a labour of love. So it has been. These have been the best years for me, the golden years. I have had a full reward in a thousand happy days on the fells....

If Starling Dodd had been the last walk of all for me, and

this the last book, I should now be desolate indeed, like a lover who has lost his loved one, and the future would have the bleakness of death. I have long known this and anticipated it, and sought desperately in my mind for some new avenue along which I could continue to express my devotion to Lakeland within the talents available to me. I am in better case than the lover who has lost his loved one, for my beloved is still there and faithful, and if there were to be a separation the defection would be mine. But why need this be the last book? Within a year I shall be retired from work (on account of old age!), but I can still walk, still draw, still write; and love itself is never pensioned off... so there must be other books....

The fleeting hour of life of those who love the hills is quickly spent, but the hills are eternal. Always there will be the lonely ridge, the dancing beck, the silent forest; always there will be the exhilaration of the summits. These are for the seeking, and those who seek and find while there is yet time will be blessed both in mind and body.

I wish you all many happy days on the fells in the years ahead.

There will be fair winds and foul, days of sun and days of rain. But enjoy them all.

Good walking! And don't forget—watch where you are putting your feet.